Lincol...

Emma
fischel ★

nosy
crow

HAGGFIEND

Flo

Hetty

Grandma

Mum

Ghoul

Forest
Pixie

Urban
Troll

First published 2015 by Nosy Crow Ltd
The Crow's Nest, Baden Place, Crosby Row
London SE1 1YW
www.nosycrow.com

ISBN: 978 0 85763 424 5

A CIP catalogue record for this book is available from the British Library.

Printed and bound in the UK by Clays Ltd, St Ives Plc.
Typeset by Tiger Media, Bishops Stortford, Hertfordshire

Papers used by Nosy Crow are made from wood grown in
sustainable forests.

3 5 7 9 8 6 4

www.nosycrow.com

For Anita of the riverbank.
Witchmum, witchgran,
and much more besides.

Thank you for everything... xx

A NOTE
TO ALL
WITCHKIDS

Araknawitchery comes easy to some witchkids. They point their fingers and – WHOOSH! – out shoots strong sticky thread, lots of it. And those witchkids can build neat, tidy webs – funnel webs, orb webs, tangle webs, all sorts.

Not me. My thread is always spindly, and my webs are a mess. But you know what? There are things I am good at. Like playing the firkelhorn, and keeping other witchkids' secrets.

And I suppose that's what this book is all about. About the horrible hairy Haggfiend and the book of mythical creatures that all turned out to be real – but also about accepting who you are as a witchkid. Being true to yourself.

Because, through all the tricky times I had – with my friends, with the sneaky witchgirl who tried to turn them against me, with the Haggfiend – one thing I learnt was this.

I canNOT pretend to be a witchgirl I'm not, and I don't want to pretend. I'm me. And I try to be the best me I can.

As for the Haggfiend, she's gone now. BUT – there are other creatures in Magical Myths of the Witchenlands. All just as scary as the Haggfiend...

And a word of warning for you Shiverlands witchkids too. Maybe you're chuckling as you read the Shiverlands Sagas. Chuckling at the Ogress of Gluggen batch-baking witchkids. Thinking she's not real, thinking you're safe.

But are you sure about that? REALLY sure?

Because if the Magical Myths all turned out to be true, then so could your Sagas – and so could the Fables of the Farflungs, and the Narrowlands Narratives...

Anyway, sleep tight, witchkids – wherever you are. But remember this. Some of those creatures attack under cover of darkness. So maybe keep one ear open.

Just in case.

Florence Skritchett

Part
One

Chapter 1

I'm Flo – Florence – Skritchett, and I live in Haggspit, capital of South Witchenland. The morning this story starts, I was woken up by loud shrieks. Mumshrieks, coming from the kitchen.

And I had a good idea what might be making Mum shriek…

Grandma.

I was right. I ran into the kitchen and found Mum, clutching on to the breakfast bar, and gnashing her teeth at Grandma. "No, Mother," Mum was shrieking. "NO!"

I didn't blame Mum for shrieking. Because,

usually, Mum's kitchen is gleaming and shiny and neat. Well, except for Grandma's corner, which is full of spellbooks and cobwebs, and a big set of cauldrons.

But now Mum's kitchen was NOT gleaming and shiny and neat. Not at all.

Because Grandma has just come back from her holidays: a week in Frakkenwild, in the Narrowlands. And Grandma's suitcase – very big, very bulky – was unpacking itself in the middle of the kitchen.

Things were flying out of it. Dumping themselves on Mum's sparkling flagstone floor, on her worktops, wherever they felt like.

All sorts of things. A half-eaten sandwich. Three enormous rocks. A spotty beach ball. A big black swimming costume and a soggy towel. Flip-flops, books, Grandma's passport – and sand and pebbles. *Lots* of sand and pebbles, all skidding around Mum's kitchen floor.

"Mother!" Mum shrieked again. "My kitchen!"

"Kristabel," said Grandma sternly. "Stop shrieking. I arrived back late last night. LATE. As you well know."

Yes. We all knew. We all heard.

Because Grandma came back very late. Around two. She came in, singing the Frakkenwild colony anthem. Woke Mum to tell her she was back, then told Mum – loudly – *all* about her holiday.

About the good bits: seeing the sound and light show at the Enchanted Glades, spotting a shoal of mergrindles in the Southern Wildwaters. About the bad bits: her nose getting sunburnt, being bitten by wizzels at night. Then Grandma went off and started crashing about in her bedroom.

Grandma is NOT a quiet sort of grandma. Not a docile grandma. Not a grandma who snoozes by the fire, and bakes, and knits scarves for forest pixies.

No.

Now Grandma was frowning at Mum. "I *must* unpack my suitcase, Kristabel," she said. "I couldn't possibly unpack it last night – it was far too late. Which is why I am unpacking it NOW."

"But not here, Mother," shrieked Mum. "Not *here*!"

It was no good. Now big black robes came flying out of Grandma's suitcase. Long black robes – olden-days robes – which is what Grandma always wears.

Muddy robes. *Very* muddy.

I gaped. So did Mum. She stopped shrieking, and staggered backwards on to a breakfast stool. "Mother," she said, faintly, "what did you *do* in Frakkenwild?"

9

"Nothing much, Kristabel," Grandma said. "Just a little relaxing hiking." Then she grinned her gappy grin at Mum, and did her innocent old witchlady look...

Which meant Grandma had been up to something.

Mum was looking alarmed now, and suspicious – both at once. "Mother," she said. "Did you remember what you promised? No law breaking? Did you remember?"

Because breaking laws is something Grandma does a LOT.

Grandma pretended to be deaf, which is also something Grandma does a lot. Especially when Mum asks her questions she doesn't want to answer.

Then Grandma waved her wand – because, yes, she has a wand. An old-style wand... Grandma will NOT use a spellstick.

"*Abrakkida Porrit, Vestirikkon Arrik,*" she said. "*Akwattik, Lavattik, Redune.*" A sprinkle of stardust whooshed out of her wand – and the robes shot off into the sink, scattering mud as they went.

Boiling-hot water came spurting from the taps. Big foaming bubbles filled the sink, and the robes began swooshing about. Washing themselves, slopping suds and bubbles and water all over Mum's floor.

Mum was slumped now, head in hands, as the robes busied themselves washing and rinsing. Then they hurled themselves out of the sink, and started wringing themselves out. Whizzing themselves round and round and round, spraying water drops all over the kitchen.

Mum's teeth started to grind. "Mother," she hissed. "There is no *need* to wandwash your robes."

Then she strode across the kitchen, dodging the robes, still spinning, still spraying. She pointed. "See this, Mother?" she said – and her voice was getting very high and very loud now. "This machine is a witchwasher. A *witchwasher*! As I have explained to you before, Mother. *Before*. Quite a few times!"

Then Mum flung the door open. "Your robes go in here, Mother. *Here*," she said. "Just as mine are about to."

Then Mum's fingers went flying on her spellstick – and a whole lot of robes zoomed through the kitchen doorway and into the witchwasher.

"See, Mother?" said Mum. "The door shuts. And the witchwasher starts. Like this. THIS! No mess. No fuss. And NO SUDS!"

Grandma snorted. "My robes are wandwash *only*, Kristabel," she said proudly. Then she glared at Mum. "And Kristabel," she said, "my magic mirror is no longer in the sitting room. Why on earth not?"

"Because…" said Mum, through gritted teeth, "it is *illegal* to have a magic mirror. You'll be arrested."

Grandma puffed up her chest. "Me? Arrested? No, no, no, Kristabel – I am *far* too important to be arrested. I am a Government Adviser! I have my own office in Argument House. I have a team! I have *staff*!"

Well, yes, Grandma *is* a government adviser. About ghouls.

Because, not long ago, Grandma spotted ghouls were about to attack Haggspit. Which was a VERY good thing because that gave us time to get rid of them. And if we hadn't, every single one of you witchkids reading this would be a ghoul by now.

But since then, Grandma has been Government Adviser on Ghouls – and also got a bit big for her boots, if you ask me.

"Kristabel," Grandma said firmly, "I shall return my magic mirror to its rightful place. Which is ON THE SITTING ROOM WALL."

Just then, a huge thunderclap boomed out. It shook the whole house, the back door flew open – and a big green box shot in.

The box landed with a thud on the kitchen worktop. A leather box, dark green, with a gold coat of arms stamped on the front. The Hovelhagg coat of arms – royal rulers of United Witchenlands for hundreds of years.

And, in big gold lettering on the front, it said this:

TOP SECRET
GOVERNMENT PROPERTY
THUNDERBOLT DELIVERY

Grandma strutted over to the worktop. "My government green box," she said importantly. "Full of vital information for a government adviser on ghouls."

She picked up the green box. "And now, Kristabel, I have work to do," she said. "Reports to study. Meetings to prepare for. Staff to instruct. Ghoul-traps to approve. If I am needed, I shall be in my room."

Then she strutted out of the kitchen.

Chapter 2

"Flo," said Mum, "I shall be out this morning. I am off to the grand opening of the Hurlstruk Happy Home."

Hurlstruk Happy Home… I saw it on our local witchscreen show, *Haggnews*, yesterday.

It's something to do with Mr Potions2Go, Meristo Hurlstruk. He's setting up an orphanage. Calling it the Hurlstruck Happy Home. Giving the little orphans lovely rooms, and the Hurlstruk surname, and opportunities like his own witchchildren have. And he was opening it right here in Haggspit.

Mum was dabbing her eyes. "The Happy Home... Such a moving idea. And today, those lucky *lucky* little orphans will move in, and I will be there to see it!"

Just then her skychatter rang. Mum snatched it up. "Miranda," she said. "What news? What news?"

Mum is a businesswitch. Runs a magazine called *Hocus Pocus*. She's rich, powerful, and successful, and Miranda works for her. But whatever Miranda's news was, it was making Mum look fed up.

"No," Mum hissed. "How did *Scoop!* find out, Miranda? How?"

Oh. Problems with *Scoop!* – again.

Scoop! is Mum's biggest rival. And right now, it's selling more copies than *Hocus Pocus*.

Mum was swirling round the kitchen – which is how Mum moves. She swirls. She strides. She marches. She hardly EVER just walks.

"Leave no stone unturned, Miranda!" Mum was saying. "Send out more witchpaps. Dig, Miranda. Dig! This time it must be us – US – who gets the exclusive!"

Mum is *always* trying to get an exclusive. Which – I think – means finding out a bit of celebrity gossip before *Scoop!* does.

Now Mum threw herself down at the kitchen table. "*Scoop!* did it AGAIN," she hissed. "An exclusive! Eleven of the top-secret *Celebrity WitchWatch* names!"

Oh.

Maybe you know about *Celebrity WitchWatch*. It's on in lots of colonies. A witchscreen show – a very boring one, in my opinion – that happens once every year.

Twelve witchcelebs all living together in a big cave-style house. Filmed day and night for two weeks. Then, in week three, the public start voting witchcelebs off the show – biggest idiot first – until there's a winner.

The new series of *Celebrity WitchWatch* is on very soon, here in South Witchenland. And usually the names of the witchcelebs taking part are kept top secret before the first show – but not this time. This time it looked like *Scoop!* had the exclusive. All but one of the names…

And Mum was NOT happy.

"Flo," she said. "We must get that final name! An exclusive! Before *Scoop!* does!"

Then I heard wailing. Wailing from across the hallway. Loud wailing. Which could only be one thing.

Hetty.
My sister. A witchteen.

Sure enough, Hetty stomped into the kitchen, wailing.

"It is over!" she wailed. "I have to face it! My time as Hero Hetty, celebrity witchteen, is OVER!"

She flung herself on a breakfast stool. Sat there, gnashing her teeth at me and Mum. "For the last two weeks I have opened my curtains," she wailed, "and do you know how many witchpaps have been outside? Trying to get a picture of me? None! NONE!"

I had no idea why Hetty was so upset. Because witchpaps, lots of them, have been hiding in the bushes around our house for weeks. And witchpaps are annoying. They lurk – all with big witchpappers slung round their necks – all waiting, all trying to get pictures of Skritchetts. And they go snooping through our bins, and shouting through our letterbox. One even chased me down the road, shouting questions at me about ghouls.

Because Grandma first spotted the ghouls, but it was all of us Skritchetts, working together, who stopped them. Including me and Hetty.

In fact, me and Hetty were headlines. Including this one:

FEARLESS FLO
AND HERO HETTY
FOIL GHOUL ATTACK!

But that headline was wrong. Because maybe Hetty was a hero – but I was *not* fearless. I was full of fear. And I do NOT like being headlines, and I do NOT like witchpaps. So I was glad they were gone...

Unlike Hetty.

Hetty slumped, still gnashing her teeth and wailing. "Fame!" she wailed. "I was *born* to be famous. My life is *pointless* if I am not famous! My life is OVER!"

Then her skychatter beeped, and she checked it. "Gigi," she said, her eyes lighting up. "Gigi has *News!*"

Gigi ... Hetty's best friend. But whatever Gigi's news was, it was NOT good news. Because Hetty took one look, and she started wailing again.

"Calamity!" she wailed. "Calamity! The government has CHANGED the law! Look! Look!" Then she showed me the headline:

NOSE-JOB POTIONS
BANNED FOR UNDER-19s
"TOO MUCH PRESSURE
ON YOUNG WITCHES
TO LOOK GOOD,"
SAY GOVERNMENT.

Oh. A nose-job potion is, for some reason, Hetty's dearest wish for her sixteenth birthday.

"Nineteen," she wailed. "THAT's how old I have to be – nineteen! But how can I wait? How can I? With a nose like this? THIS! So tiny, so neat, so straight! How *can* I?"

Now smoke was pouring out of Hetty's ears, in big sudden bursts, which always happens when she's upset. "Stupid government!" she wailed. "Saying there's too much pressure on young witches to look good. There's no pressure. NONE! I just *need* a better nose! A truly witchy nose! One with lovely big lumps and bumps!"

Then Mum swirled over. "Hetty, shush, I have something for you," she said. Then she waved a ticket in Hetty's face…

THE WARTS
ADMIT ONE

The Warts – the Witchscreen Arts awards ceremony. Where hundreds of witchscreen celebrities all gather together, wearing posh robes. Then they eat some dinner, and give out lots of prizes.

And it was happening tonight.

Hetty stopped wailing. Snatched the ticket off Mum, stared – and started screeching. "It's for the Pen," she screeched. "The *Pen*!"

The Pen is a closed-off bit at the front of the Warts. Full of witchteens, standing and screaming up at the stars on stage.

"I used my contacts," beamed Mum. "Got you a ticket. So tonight, darling," she said, patting Hetty on the head, "you have a chance of finding a boyfriend. Possibly even a *celebrity* boyfriend!"

Then Mum swirled off.

Hetty's eyes were shining. Because a boyfriend is something Hetty is longing for.

"This is it, Flo," she gasped. "My big chance. The Pen! A good place to find a boyfriend! An excellent place!"

Then her fingers went flying on her witchfixer. She gasped more. "And maybe Mum is right. Maybe a *celebrity* boyfriend!" she said. "Because Kakkle Kru are playing!"

I looked. Kakkle Kru. Witchboys – five of them

– all with floppy hair and big mouths. Hetty jabbed a finger at one of them. "Jekyll," she screeched. "Maybe it will be Jekyll."

Then she started nodding confidently. "Yes," she said. "Most probably it will be Jekyll. After all, we have a LOT in common. Because the witchpaps may be gone but I am *still* Hero Hetty – a celebrity myself. And us witchcelebs should stick together. We understand the *pressures* of fame!"

Then she charged out of the kitchen, across the hallway, and off to her bedroom. I heard the door slam shut – and then, the front doorbell rang.

Chapter 3

I ran to answer the door. I knew who it would be – Kika. Kika Rorrit-Mogg. One of my two best friends.

I opened the door, and Kika hurled herself at me. "Flo!" she screeched. "It has been SO long!"

Well, actually, it had been two weeks. Because Kika has been away, visiting her dad's family in Taklik. Which, if you don't know, is one of the Farflungs – those five small islands way down in the Serpent Sea.

I went away, too. To our holiday villa, on the coast at Kronebay where South Witchenland meets

Witchenfinn. But we only had a week there, because Mum had to get back for work.

We packed a lot into that week, though. We trekked on three-humped dongladrons. We had a picnic by the Wailing Waterfalls. And on the last day, Mum did a transforming spell, and we spent all day being mermaids.

Kika stopped the hugging and stepped back. Then she whipped something out of her pocket. "What do you think, Flo?" she beamed. "My new look. What do you think?"

I gaped.

Kika had just stuck a pair of specs on her nose.

Nothing surprising about that – lots of witchkids wear specs. But Kika's were very big, very purple and shaped up at the sides like pointy wings. They had little crystals – twinkling and shining – studded all along the arms. And they covered half her face.

"Oversized and glamorous, with butterfly frames," Kika said proudly, beaming out from behind them. "The perfect choice for my face shape."

Then she clasped my arm. "Because, Flo," she said, "if you have a square face with a strong jaw, like I do – you can afford to go dramatic. Making butterfly frames the perfect choice."

23

Then she beamed. "Page seventy-one," she said. "*Choosing specs that suit.*"

Page 71 of the Book.

The Book is something Kika gave my other best friend, Lily, for her last birthday. *Two Hundred Utterly Important Things a Witchgirl Should Know.* Which was a lie, as none of it was utterly important, not to me.

But ALL of it was utterly important to Lily and Kika. And Kika found it *so* utterly important, she bought herself a copy too. Now she hardly ever talks without quoting the Book.

Kika was looking around, frowning. "Where are the witchpaps, Flo?" she said.

"They've gone," I said.

"Gone?" gasped Kika. "Gone?"

"Yes," I said.

Kika looked concerned. "Poor Flo," she said. "Your sudden stardom – gone!" She patted my arm. "Sometimes, Flo, there will be difficult times in your life. Times when things aren't going your way. Times—"

"Kika," I said. "Shush. This is NOT a difficult time. This is a good time. I am *glad* the witchpaps are gone."

And I was. I really was.

★

Me and Kika both live near the very top of Moaning Mountain, in Upper Haggspit. We set off from my house to walk down to Lily's.

Lily Jaggwort, my other best friend.

Lily lives further down Moaning Mountain, near the edge of Upper Haggspit. Usually it takes about twenty minutes to walk to Lily's house. But not today. Today it took almost forty – because of Kika. She was SO slow.

It was her shoes. I was too busy noticing the specs to notice the shoes at first. But I noticed them now.

They were very sparkly – but also very clumpy. With heels like fat wedges of kronkel-milk cheese. And so heavy it was a big effort for Kika to even lift her feet off the ground.

It wasn't just Kika's shoes that slowed her down. It was also her robes. Which were short, stripy, and tight – extremely tight.

So, what with the shoes and the robes, all Kika could manage was to totter, with tiny wobbling steps.

"Hurry *up*," I said.

"Flo," said Kika, struggling. "Do these shoes, and my on-trend stripy bandage robe, look like the sort of outfit a witchgirl can hurry in?"

"You should wear flat shoes then," I grumbled.

"And looser robes. I am, and look – I can stride. I can run. I can jump."

And I showed her. I started striding, broke into a run, and jumped right over a boggle-poop bin.

But Kika just threw back her head and did a tittering sort of cackle. "Flats, Flo?" she tittered. "Looser robes? I think NOT!"

Then she shrieked, as a swarm of tiny zizzwings flew past – all buzzing and turning from bright blue to bright green to bright yellow as they flew.

Still – *at last* – we got there. Kika tottered the last few steps to Lily's house. And Lily flung open the door before we even rang the bell. "Hi!" she shrieked. "Hi!"

Because Lily also went away for two weeks. To Lakktarn in the Narrowlands.

There was a LOT of shrieking after that. Kika shrieking at Lily. Lily shrieking back. Both of them shrieking at me – and the three of us jumping around in a big group hug.

"Back with my witchbesties," beamed Lily. "I am *so* happy!"

I was gaping. Something was different about Lily.

Lily has grown a lot lately, and her legs have done most of the growing, so they're long and skinny, like pelloligan legs. And her face is long and skinny too, with huge round eyes. But right now – she had long black fake eyelashes.

"Kika, Flo," said Lily, batting those eyelashes. "What do you think? Super-stylish?"

"Definitely," said Kika, nodding hard. "Super-stylish. Definitely."

I wasn't entirely sure they *were* super-stylish. They looked a bit like spiders to me. And anyway, I had something I wanted to ask Lily.

Because Lily and her mum stayed in a hotel near the Churnings, the Fourth Wonder of Witchworld. And I really *really* want to see the Churnings – see all those vast crashing waves. Those waves that roll over and over in the Wildwaters but never come to shore. Those giant waves, with glimpses – if you're lucky – of sea creatures found nowhere else in the whole of Witchworld.

"So – what were they like? The Churnings?" I said.

"Oh … big, rolly," said Lily vaguely. Then she grabbed me and Kika by the arm. "And now," she said proudly, "I have something to show you."

✦

I stood in the doorway of Lily's bedroom and gaped. It was all different. Last time I was here, it was full of Destiny Daggett stuff.

Destiny Daggett – fearless witchkid who roams Witchworld sorting out villains in *Skyhunter*. Our favourite witchscreen show.

Last time Lily had a Destiny Daggett dartboard. A Destiny Daggett duvet set. A Destiny Daggett poster. And a pinboard with lots of Destiny Daggett stuff pinned to it.

Not any more. There was no Destiny Daggett anywhere. It was all gone. Even the duvet had changed. No Destiny Daggett – instead some flowery, swirly patterns, and a small fluffy rug by her bed. Her pinboard was covered with pictures of witchscreen stars and witchboy bands.

The whole room was twinkling with little sparkling green lights. And on Lily's desk, she had a mirror with lights all round the edge. And a stack of boxes with little compartments for jewellery. And a small fluffy rug by her bed.

"Page seventy-eight," Lily said proudly. "*Turn your bedroom into a boudoir.*"

Then Lily stopped. Listened.

We all listened – because we could all hear it. A low moaning sound. A moaning, groaning sound… Coming right from the heart of the mountain.

Chapter
4

Every witchkid who lives on Moaning Mountain knows what to do if the mountain moans. There are big signs everywhere:

**IF THE MOUNTAIN MOANS
LEAVE THE GROUND IMMEDIATELY.
DO NOT STOP TO COLLECT PERSONAL
BELONGINGS!**

Sometimes Haggspit council runs practice drills. The sirens go off, and all witches in Haggspit have to get off the ground.

If we're in school, we leave our classrooms and run to the schoolshuttles, then strap ourselves in, ready for take-off.

If we're not in school, we leave the ground with our grown-ups or – like now, as Lily's grown-ups weren't in – run for the nearest assembly point. Pick-up points where witches can wait for emergency skybuses to get them off the mountain.

But this was NOT a practice drill. This was the real thing. And the moaning from the mountain was getting louder.

Too loud. Much too loud.

Lily charged to her front door, hurled it open, and we ran for Assembly Point 4. Our nearest.

All around us, witches were streaming out of houses. Whole families clambering into skyriders. Shooting up into the air and away from the mountain.

"Hurry!" said Lily, rushing ahead. "HURRY!"

But hurrying was NOT something Kika could manage. Behind me, I heard her wail, then crash to the ground.

"My shoes," she wailed. "I fell off them!"

"Leave them," I said. "Kick them off!"

"Leave them?" gasped Kika. "But they might get ruined!"

I didn't bother arguing. I could feel the ground starting to quake under my feet so I just yanked her shoes off.

"I'll hold them," I said, hauling her up. "Now go!"

"Faster!" Lily yelled, halfway down the street now. "Faster! Or we'll miss it! Kika, RUN!"

But Kika could NOT run. Her robes were just too tight. She tried to run. Took tiny urgent steps, but she was still SO slow.

Too slow.

We got to Assembly Point 4 just as the skybus took off. Just as holes started appearing in the ground. Gaping holes – in back gardens, on slopes, on streets. One, then another, then another…

The Windwhirls of Moaning Mountain – First Wonder of Witchworld – were about to begin.

✳

Witchboffins argue all the time about why the mountain moans, and how windwhirls happen.

Most witchboffins think it's the hot springs bubbling in the middle of Moaning Mountain that do it. That the springs give off gases. That sometimes the springs overheat, and the gases get bigger. Then pressure builds up inside the mountain. Builds up and up and up – until the pressure gets so big, the mountain starts moaning. Then it blasts holes in itself. Big tunnels through the rock to get rid of the pressure, to get rid of the gases.

And those gases go swirling up through the big tunnels. Up and up and up. Until they hit the air and explode. And it's those explosions that create swirling whirling funnels of wind... Windwhirls.

Not all witchboffins think that's the reason windwhirls happen – but whatever the reason, they were happening right now.

Roaring noises – deafening, terrifying noises – were coming from deep in the mountain. The roaring of things hurtling towards the surface.

Then—

BOOM! BOOM! BOOM! BOOM! BOOM!

One after another, the gases shot out of the mountain and exploded. Boomed out, loud as thunderclaps. Then formed swirling whirling funnels of wind.

I was panicking. Really panicking.

Because I've seen windwhirls before – but never from the ground. And never ones as big as these. These were the biggest windwhirls I had EVER seen.

Vast funnels of wind – the size of tower blocks. Green funnels, blue funnels, orange and red and purple funnels. Funnels of every colour you can think of streaking across the sky.

Swirling, twisting windwhirls. Swooping and swerving, twisting and turning and roaring. Scooping up everything in their path…

Including me and Lily and Kika.

It was like being sucked into the mouth of a monster.

I clung on to Lily, to Kika. Thundering noises roared in my ears. I felt dizzy. Helpless. Swirling round and round, like robes in a witchwasher. And all around us other things were swirling. Branches, bits of roof, bits of flexipod, a boggle, a windsniffer… All lurching and bucketing, swirling and spinning. All helpless. All trapped. Spinning round and round and round.

And then we were falling. Me, Lily, Kika, all spinning and spiralling, down and down and down through the swirling funnel of wind.

Then it dropped us. We were out – and the windwhirl roared on.

Out…

But NOT on the ground.

No.

Nowhere near the ground.

Up as high as we could possibly be. Up at the

highest point in Haggspit. So high I could see the whole of Haggspit spread out below me.

Up at the very top of Moaning Mountain – and clinging on.

Clinging on to the head of a statue. A statue that towers over the whole of Haggspit Harbour. The tallest, scariest statue in the whole of Haggspit.

The top half – the worst, most vicious of sorceresses. Huge head thrown back, snarling mouth wide open in a scream. One long bony arm stretched out, and pointing.

The bottom half – all fiend. Huge and strong, with thundering hooves. And a long curving tail with a spike on the end…

The statue of the Haggfiend. With me, Kika, Lily – all clinging on. Terrified.

Chapter 5

I clung on. Wedged on the Haggfiend's huge hooked nose. Squashed between two big bony bumps.

I could see Lily – stuck where the Haggfiend's shoulder met her neck. Tucked right in. Not looking out. Not looking down.

And Kika dangling below me. Dangling – upside down – off one of the Haggfiend's coiling, snaky ringlets of hair. Hanging on by her legs.

And shrieking.

"I totally do NOT believe it!" shrieked Kika, panicking and wriggling. "It is not *possible*! How can I be stuck – UPSIDE DOWN – on the

Haggfiend's hair?"

"Kika," I said. "Pull yourself up. You *can*. Pretend you're on a trapeze. Doing the bat impression. Pull yourself up, just like you did then."

Because me and Kika and Lily used to do bat impressions. All hanging upside down off the trapeze in her garden.

"Pretend I'm on a trapeze? Doing the bat impression?" Kika shrieked. "I am NOT on a trapeze doing a bat impression. I am upside down on the Haggfiend's hair. Upside down on a statue – a *magistatue*! And right now it is IMPOSSIBLE to pretend I am anywhere else!"

And just then – the statue moved.

Slowly, slowly, it swivelled its huge stone head. Swivelled its huge stone body. Swivelled its long outstretched arm, and turned to point and stare out over Witchenwater.

"Nooooo!" shrieked Kika, almost falling off. "Why *now*? Why did this stupid *stupid* magistatue have to move NOW? When we are STUCK on it? Why? It is not *fair*!"

Well, I agreed. It *wasn't* fair.

Because the statue only moves twice a day. At two random moments. So it was VERY unlucky it happened right now.

Kika was sobbing now. Sobbing and shrieking. "Haggfiend Horror!" she sobbed. "This is our very own Haggfiend Horror! A real-life Haggfiend Horror!"

Because the Haggfiend is from a terrifying myth. A myth called "Haggfiend Horror". In a famous book, *Magical Myths of the Witchenlands*.

Then Lily spoke, in a small, wobbling voice. "Flo, Kika, there are three hundred and seventy-six steps up the side of Haggspit Heights to the Haggfiend statue," she said. "I have climbed every one of those steps on three occasions. I have looked up at this statue from the ground. But I am now looking up at this statue from its shoulder. And I am looking straight up its nostril. Which is a hole about as big as my head."

Then Lily buried her face in the cold metal of one stringy neck tendon. "This statue is over thirty metres tall," she said miserably. "It weighs about the same as one hundred double-decker skyshuttles. It is big and grey and ugly and scary – and I am NOT happy being this high up, and this close to its screaming mouth."

She buried her head more. "Particularly as no one will save us."

I had a horrible feeling Lily was right.

The Haggfiend statue is the first thing witches see as they fly along Skyway 1 over Witchenwater. The screaming face, the long arm, pointing. Stretching out, into the distance – like she's reaching to grab something with her bony hand.

It's one of the most famous landmarks in South Witchenland. A landmark that witches *ooh* and *aah* over every day. But right now, I knew just how many witches would be *ooh*ing and *aah*ing over the Haggfiend statue.

None.

I could see witches returning to the ground now the windwhirls were over. Skyriders landing. Tiny specks on the ground. Witches on skychatters. Checking where their families were. *Not* checking for tiny specks on the Haggfiend statue.

I could see my own house. So close, so SO close. And Kika's, even closer. Just through the woods, just through the trees.

I felt for my skychatter. Tried to get it out of my robe pocket, call for help. But it fell out of my hand. And I watched as it fell and fell and fell – then smashed on the ground far below.

"Did you see that?" shrieked Kika. "How long that took! How far it fell! How it SMASHED! That will be us in a minute. US!"

"Flo, Kika," said Lily, her face totally buried in the stone now. "I canNOT look. I canNOT move. Because if I move I am going to fall. Totally. And I am not at all sure I can hang on to the Haggfiend's neck for very much longer."

I wriggled forward and looked down.

"Lily," I said. "Hold on. You've got to hold on. Wait for help."

There was nothing else we could do. We couldn't climb down. It was too far, too dangerous, not enough to hold on to.

"Flo, I don't think I can wait," said Lily. "Or hold on. I don't think I can."

Lily's eyes were huge now. Her teeth were clattering. "I'm going to fall," she whimpered.

"You are NOT going to fall," I said.

I stared down at Lily from the Haggfiend's bony nose. What could I do? Could I use my belt? Loop it round Lily somehow? Slither out of my leggings? Get her to grab hold of the ends? Tie herself on somehow until help came?

No. I couldn't reach her.

She had to wait. We all had to.

And now Kika was sobbing. Really sobbing. "I can't pull myself up," she sobbed. "I'm too scared. It's too high. Too far to fall."

Then her teeth started clacking. "And I'm cold," she said. "It's so cold."

Which it was. This high up, it was way colder than down on the ground.

"And it's gusty," said Lily in a muffled voice, her face buried. "Very gusty. And gusty is not good."

"Lily, Kika," I said. "We *have* to hold on. Someone will see us. They WILL."

"They won't," Kika sobbed.

Now Lily was going paler and paler, starting to sway.

"Lily, hang on," I said.

"Flo," she said, looking up, looking terrified. "I feel … dizzy. My fingers… I'm losing my grip."

And that's when I saw it. Out of the corner of my eye.

A small black speck zooming up out of the woods. A small black speck that looked like a bird – but wasn't. I knew who it was.

Grandma.

Getting nearer and nearer, holding her broomstick with one hand, and brandishing her wand with the other.

"*Abrakkida Sillik!*" I heard her shout. "*Kaperikk Non Pillik! Dekkidik Dekkodik, Arune!*"

A shower of stardust shot out of the end of her

wand, then a shimmering shape began to appear. Flat and purple and swooping towards us…

Just as Lily's fingers lost their grip and she started to fall.

Chapter
6

A magicreation – a temporary magic creation. That's what Grandma did.

A magicreation of a flying carpet. A wide purple carpet that came swirling towards us. Scooped Lily up as she went tumbling. Then hovered by the statue while Kika dropped down from the Haggfiend's hair, and I jumped down from the Haggfiend's nose.

Then Grandma's magicreation flew us all home – first Lily, then Kika, then me. All a bit shocked. All a bit scared.

Back home, Mum was pacing round the kitchen as I opened the back door. She turned and came hurtling towards me, ghostly green.

"Flo, where were you? Where *were* you?" she gasped. "And your skychatter – why didn't you answer it? What happened?"

"Kristabel," said Grandma calmly, marching in behind me. "Flo is perfectly safe. At least, she is now. She was, however, scooped up by a windwhirl and—"

"Scooped up?" Mum shrieked. "Scooped up by a windwhirl! SCOOPED UP?"

"Yes, Kristabel," said Grandma. "Scooped up. And the windwhirl that scooped up Flo then proceeded to *strand* Flo."

"To STRAND Flo?" shrieked Mum, even louder. "Where? *Where* did the windwhirl strand Flo?"

"At the top of the Haggfiend statue," said Grandma calmly.

Mum collapsed on to a breakfast stool. "At the top –" she gasped. "The top! But the Haggfiend statue is thirty metres high. Thirty metres!"

I thought Mum was about to faint.

"And *that*, Kristabel," said Grandma sternly, "is precisely why I need to KEEP the magic mirror. To check for Skritchetts in trouble. Like Flo."

Grandma had spotted an opportunity – and she seized it. "Now will you stop all your SILLY talk of getting rid of my magic mirror? *Now* do you understand how foolish you have been?"

"Yes, Mother," said Mum, nodding hard. "Yes. Absolutely."

Then she stared at me. "Oh Flo," Mum said, with a big wobble in her voice. "What if you had fallen? What if—"

She stopped. Leapt off her stool and rushed over to me. "Flo, you have cuts," she said, staring right in my face. "*Cuts*. And scratches."

She started biting her lip. "Anything feel broken? Any sign of fever? Concussion? Trauma? Hallucinations?"

"I feel fine, Mum," I said. "Just a bit … well, shocked. But my skychatter – it fell out of my robes. It smashed on the ground. And my keys. They've gone too. They must have fallen out in the windwhirl."

"Skychatters … keys … those we can replace," Mum said, hugging me. "But you, Flo, you – strange little Skritchett that you are, with the most peculiar hobbies, and absolutely no sense of witchwear style – I can NOT replace you."

★

Mum calmed down after a bit. Then made me a mug of hot glimberry juice. "This is what you need," she said, squirting a big blob of kronkel-cream on the top. "A hot drink. A rest. And you'll feel much better."

Then her skychatter rang and she snatched it up. "Miranda," she said. "What news? Any clues?" And off she swirled, hissing – and I heard her office door slam shut.

I took the glimberry juice to my bedroom. Curled up in my favourite spot. My den – the cosy space below my bed. Glad to be home. Glad to be safe.

My den has a wall of pictures at one end. Pictures I look at every single day. Lots and lots of pictures. Mostly pictures of Dad. Me and Dad.

Dad. My missing dad.

He's been missing more than two whole years…

Too long. *Much* too long.

In that time I have grown two inches taller. My feet are two sizes bigger. I have cut my hair in a new shape. I have learnt to use a wand. I have saved Witchworld from a ghoul attack. I have ridden a broomstick.

But Dad knows nothing about any of it.

I saw Dad go missing. Saw him fighting to save me from a huge snarling ghoul. Saw him and the ghoul, both trapped, both struggling. Both hooked to each other, by the ghoul's curved claws…

And both hooked to a rocket, a giant GIANT rocket. Dad trapped, the ghoul trapped. Hooked to a rocket that screeched up into the sky. A rocket that exploded – right over the Ice Volcano.

Grandma says Lyle Skritchett – my dad – could survive a ghoul, and a rocket, and an Ice Volcano. Grandma says one day we'll get some sign he survived. Or maybe he'll just walk in through the door.

And I believe Grandma is right. I *do*. But over two years is a VERY long time, and some days – especially lately – I believe a bit less.

I sniffed. I couldn't help it.

Dad didn't live with me – but I saw him lots, stayed with him lots. Sometimes with Hetty, sometimes without. And each time he came to collect me, I ran to open the front door and he'd scoop me up.

"News, Flo," Dad would say, in his big booming voice. "Tell me your News."

And today I had big News. Astonishing News. News that would amaze him.

So I rubbed my eyes. Then I looked at my pictures…

Me. A witchbaby-me. Small and round, with one tuft of black hair. Sitting on Dad's lap. On holiday in Drakken, up in the Shiverlands, waving one small fat hand at a family of sea serpents whooshing past.

Me and Dad, both dressed as dragons, ready for the Haggspit fancy-dress parade.

Me and Dad squashed into an armchair. Me holding a big book – green and gold…

Magical Myths of the Witchenlands.

A book full of myths translated from Ancient Witchspeak into Witchen. Myths from every colony in the United Witchenlands. From South Witchenland, Witchenfinn, Witchenwild, Witchenwail – all of them.

Myths about all sorts of creatures. Deadly dodgers and honkbottles. The Dromedangler and the Globegobbler. Dredgeboggles, and hootwaggles, and the seven-tusked Oglestomp.

Spinetingling stories. Bloodcurdling stories. Stories that made me gasp. Stories that made me laugh. Some funny, some disgusting – and some truly terrifying…

Like "Haggfiend Horror".

And that picture, the one of me and Dad, squashed in the armchair. I remember the night Dad took it. The night Dad first gave me the book, *Magical Myths of the Witchenlands*.

I remember it clear as clear…

47

Chapter 7

That night it was dark outside, and cold. Rain lashed against the windows. Wind howled round the house. And me and Dad were squashed into his armchair. He called it his story armchair.

Every night I stayed, Dad would read to me in the story armchair at bedtime. Funny stories. Exciting stories. Stories that told me things, that explained things. All kinds of stories.

"Flo," said Dad, that dark and rainy night. "It is time we read this." And he handed me a book.

And there it was.

Magical Myths of the Witchenlands. Lots of

green, lots of gold – and a picture on the cover. A scary picture.

A witch with hair that looked all wriggly, as if it was moving and writhing. Sharp yellow teeth and cruel staring eyes. A hairy body, bristling legs, huge clomping hooves, and a long swishing tail, with a sharp pointed spike on the end…

I gasped. I was a bit thrilled – and a LOT scared.

"Daddy," I said. "Is this suitable? I am only six, and that is a very scary monster on the cover."

"Flo," said Dad. "Six is a very good age to read about monsters. Besides, these are *our* monsters. Monsters of the Witchenlands. And all defeated by witchchildren."

"Witchchildren?" I said.

"Witchchildren," said Dad, nodding his head. "Witchchildren – small in size, young in age – but BIG in brains. Witchchildren full of daring, full of courage. Clever, cunning witchchildren. Outwitting honkbottles. Trapping the Globegobbler. Defeating the Oglestomp."

"Are these stories true, Daddy?" I said, feeling doubtful. "Because I don't think it's very likely that small witchchildren could defeat big monsters."

"Flo," said Dad. "There you are wrong.

Small witchchildren are PERFECTLY capable of such things."

I looked at the cover again. "Daddy," I said. "Our statue – the big one I can just see from our garden, the one pointing and screaming at the very top of our mountain – she looks a bit like this monster."

"Our statue is this monster, Flo," said Dad. "This is the Haggfiend. The Haggspit monster. OUR monster."

"She looks an extremely bad monster," I said.

"Flo," Dad said. "She *is* an extremely bad monster. She is *dreadful*.

She is a SHOCKER. There is not one good thing I could *possibly* say about that hideous Haggfiend. She even pushes her own mother and father off a cliff!"

I gasped. "Pushes her own mother and father OFF A CLIFF?" I said.

"She does," Dad said.

Dad paused. Lowered his voice. "She has a wand that can cast deep dark enchantments. And one terrible gift, Flo. The gift of DISGUISE!"

"Disguise?" I said.

"That ghastly creature can take the shape of an *ordinary* witch. A lovely smiling witchlady," said Dad. "And off she goes, roaming. Seeking out little witchvictims. Witchgirls."

"Witchgirls?" I said, huddling closer to Dad.

"Hundreds of them," said Dad, nodding. "All scooped up and flown through the woods to her dark damp lair. All made to be her SLAVES, scurrying about the whole day long, doing the bidding of that hideous cackling creature. And the smell of her, Flo, the SMELL —"

AGGFIEND

"Daddy," I said. "You are actually scaring

me. I think you should stop now."

"Scaring you?" Dad said. Then he shook his head and smiled down at me. "There's no need to be scared, Flo. None at all. Because the Haggfiend – all these monsters – are *myths*. NOT real. They do not exist."

Then Dad sighed. "How sad it is that these monsters are myths. No chance to actually MEET one of them. To find a deadly dodger snoozing under the bed. Or a thrumbulger curled up in the wardrobe. To answer the doorbell, and find a honkbottle wiping its huge paws on the doormat."

Dad looked at me, eyes gleaming. "So listen and shiver and thrill, Flo," he said. "Shiver and thrill, because you know you are *safe*. From the Haggfiend. From ALL the monsters in this book."

Then Dad got out his skychatter. "And let us remember this moment, Flo," he said. "The day you first read about the Haggfiend. Our very own monster."

Then he clicked his skychatter, took the picture, and began to read.

✶

I will never forget how I felt. How safe I felt squashed in Dad's story armchair, with Dad's arm around me. How I shivered and thrilled, how my spine tingled, as Dad read the words.

Words I have read again and again and again ever since. Words I know so well.

And now, today, I sat, holding the picture close. Me and Dad, curled up in the story armchair. Remembering.

Then I sniffed. Rubbed my eyes. *Again.*

One day Dad will hear ALL my News…

One day.

Chapter 8

The windwhirls were the top story on *Haggnews* that evening. The biggest, strongest windwhirls ever measured. Sweeping through the whole of Haggspit, past the Singing Stillwaters, then north as far as the edges of Gormwitt. And they did a LOT of damage.

Me and Grandma sat in the kitchen watching *Haggnews*. A witchboffin was talking about why the windwhirls were so big, so strong. Saying maybe witchglobe warming was the problem. Us witches filling the air with skyriders, using more and more magic supplies, making the witchglobe hotter and hotter.

Then Mum came swirling in, dressed for the Warts. Dark-crimson robes, long and shimmering, swishing on the flagstones as she swirled, talking into her skychatter.

"Yes, Miranda," she was saying, sounding thrilled. "Agorikka Glimp! Producer of *Celebrity WitchWatch*! At my table tonight! This is my big chance to discuss the show. Get the exclusive! Find out the name of the twelfth witchceleb. Who will it be? Who?"

Behind Mum, Hetty came clacking, eyes shining. Hair piled high, like a three-storey bird's nest. With purple eyes, and purple lips, and robes that were mostly purple spots. Towering on shiny red shoes.

"Flo," said Mum, sweeping over to me and holding my shoulders, "if you have any problems, any symptoms – any AT ALL – call me. I will come straight back."

"I'll be fine, Mum," I said.

"And, Mother," said Mum, looking sternly at Grandma as a skycab landed outside. "I am trusting you to behave. Flo has had a traumatic and shocking experience today, so no doing anything silly."

"Fear not, Kristabel," said Grandma. "Flo and I will enjoy a quiet night together, tackling this."

She held out a box. A 5000-piece jigsaw. A

picture of Haggspit Harbour.

Grandma was lying.

Five minutes later Grandma's biggest cauldron was bubbling and steaming, and flames were leaping in the heavy metal grate plonked in the middle of Mum's kitchen floor.

And there were frogs. Frogs *everywhere*. Frogs bounding and skidding across the floor. Frogs splashing in the cauldron. Frogs hopping along the worktops.

There were jars too. Open jars, lots of them. Jars with labels in Grandma's spidery writing…

NIBBET NIGHTMARES
STRIGGLE SNEEZES
OGRE DAYDREAMS
WITCHBABY BURBLES
DRIED SWAMPSLUDGE

And one jar with a big heavy lid, and a label that caught my eye…

STINKING IDLEWORT

"No, Grandma," I said. "You can't use stinking idlewort. Not in here. Not in Mum's kitchen."

Grandma's eyes popped. "I most certainly can, Flo. And I *must*. Every truth potion must have stinking idlewort."

"Truth potion?" I said. "*Why* are you making truth potion?"

"Because of Ariadne Von Trinkpott!" Grandma said. "Welfare Witchminister. I believe she is lying. Claiming money – from *our* government, Flo, paid out of *our* taxes – that she should NOT be claiming. I shall make her confess, using truth potion..."

Then she stirred the potion with a long spoon. "But first," Grandma said happily, "I am about to sort out the problem of Stink!"

I expect you already know the problem of Stink. That witches are NEVER fooled into drinking truth potion. Because of idlewort, and its Stink.

One witchman – Jeraboam Inkbold – did get rid of Stink in his truth potion. But that was long long ago, and he refused to say how he did it.

So witches are STILL trying to take Stink out of truth potion...

Like Grandma.

"If Jeraboam Inkbold managed to get rid of Stink, then so shall I!" she said.

Then she brought something out of her robe

pocket. "A little souvenir of Frakkenwild," she said, cackling.

She opened the box – just for one second – then snapped it shut.

One second was enough. I clapped my hand over my mouth. One second was enough. "Grandma, that smells DISGUSTING," I said, almost choking. "What is it?"

"Reeking stenchflox," Grandma said, with a cunning look on her face. "Fight a stink *with* a stink!"

"Grandma, are you sure it will work?" I said.

Grandma looked offended. "Are you doubting me, Flo?" she said. "Me? A Government Adviser?"

I wasn't sure Grandma being a government adviser on ghouls made her an expert on Stink in truth potion. But I had a feeling Grandma would NOT be happy if I pointed that out. So I didn't.

Grandma stirred the potion once more. "A little more simmering time," she said, "and it will be ready for those final stinking ingredients. But first – one sprig of wild disselslik."

Then she hitched up her robes and sprinted for the back door.

Chapter 9

Grandma may be eighty-three – but she can move fast. She grabbed her broomstick, flung open the door, and headed outside.

"Hop on, Flo," she said, grinning her gappy grin at me.

So I *did* hop on, right behind Grandma – and off we went. Swooping down the garden, towards the woods.

Yes, I know. I *know*. It IS against the law – at least, here in United Witchenlands it is. Article 3047 of the Witch Wellbeing and Safety Act, version 213. No under-sixteens on broomsticks.

But I am beginning to think there are too many laws for us witchkids. And some of those laws are just silly – like that one.

Because *all* witchkids should get a chance to ride a broomstick.

The witches in charge of this book would like me to make clear that any views on laws and broomsticks, as expressed here, are my own opinions, and do NOT represent the opinions of witches in the Crow's Nest. Who are extremely law-abiding witches.

I found it scary – terrifying – the first time. But not now.

Now Grandma often takes me out on her broomstick. She says it needs exercise every day. And when Grandma flies us on the small, traffic-free skyways, there's no engine, no noise, no faint smell of dragon oil. Nothing. Just silence, and clouds – and the feel of the wind whooshing through my hair.

It's a bit wobbly, and it's cold and uncomfortable, but being on a broomstick makes me feel free. Free, like I'm a soaring pelloligan. Free, like I'm part of the sky.

I love it.

I'm even learning myself – on Grandma's spare.

Today Grandma went swooping over the gate at the bottom of my garden, then swerved through the trees, down into the woods.

The woods are a wild bit of Moaning Mountain, protected from building because rare plants grow there. They stretch for miles and miles – but Grandma soon landed. She jammed her broomstick at the ground, and we both hopped off.

"Ah-hah!" Grandma said, crouching down. "Just the thing!"

She pulled up a sprig of something spindly and grey. "Wild disselslik," she said. "Crushed, then sprinkled in my potion. Perfect!"

And back we went, swooping once more through the woods, over the gate, and into the garden.

Halfway up the garden, Grandma landed. Stopped so suddenly I almost fell off.

"Listen!" she whispered, eyes gleaming.

And I did listen.

Noises were coming from somewhere in the garden. Strange noises. High-pitched noises. Small, indignant, cross-sounding noises. Somewhere between a croak and a squawk.

Crawk… Crawk… Crawk…

Grandma's eyes lit up. Then – like a windsniffer on the trail of grubbles – she started tracking. Sniffing. Tiptoeing. Creeping around the garden, trying to work out where the noises came from.

It took a while, because my garden is big, and there are a LOT of places for crawkers to hide. But we tracked them down in the end.

Round the side of the house, behind the sheds. Three sheds, all clustered together, all used to store garden stuff, one with a gripball hoop attached to its wall.

That's where they were.

Behind the sheds, where Mum puts all the junk. Stuff she hasn't got time to sort – including an old witchwasher…

I gaped.

There, inside the door of the witchwasher, leaning out of a very scruffy nest, were three babies – mainly fluffy hair and tiny round faces. All with their mouths wide open, all crawking for food…

Trolls. Baby trolls. Urban trolls.

Now, I have seen fully grown urban trolls. But not baby ones. And they were cute. So round. And *so* fluffy.

But I knew what we had to do. "Grandma, we

should tell Mum," I said.

"We should NOT tell her," said Grandma firmly, looking at the crawking babies as if they were the most marvellous things in the world.

"But Mum hates urban trolls," I said. "She says they steal. Raid the bins. She says they should stay in the wild, where they belong. She says they're pests."

Because every time Mum finds an urban troll creeping about in the garden – which happens quite often – she calls in vermin control. VapZappers, the Vermin and Pest Zappers.

Grandma snorted. "Urban trolls are NOT pests. They are *survivors*, Flo. And if trolls have become urban, it is the fault of witches. Greedy witches. Witches who destroy their forests, their food. All trolls would live in the wilds if they could. It is witches who FORCE them to become urban."

"But, Grandma, they're smelly," I said, holding my nose. Because maybe those babies smelt lovely to other urban trolls – but not to a witchkid.

"You'd be smelly if you lived in an old witchwasher," said Grandma. "Urban trolls are clean little things if they can be."

Well, that could be true – because once Mum found one in her bathroom, trying to jump up and turn her shower on, and she had to chase it out.

"But Mum says they're sly. Cunning," I said.

"They are *clever*," said Grandma, even more firmly. "Sharp as tacks. Far cleverer than other trolls."

Which – I'm sure you'll agree – is not hard. Trolls are not known for their brain power. Not desert trolls, not forest trolls. Not even the snow trolls, the ones who sing like angels. And definitely not bald trolls, the ones from the Outerlands. The ones who sit around all day, with their mouths half open, dribbling and scratching their heads – which is what makes them go bald.

The three troll babies crawked more. The one in the middle slightly bigger. Slightly bolder. The leader…

"They're hungry," Grandma said.

"They eat disgusting food, Grandma," I said. Because in the last series of *Wild and Wonderful Witchglobe* they showed all the things an urban troll ate in one year. Old rubbish. Rotting takeaways. Mouldy things.

"These trolls would happily eat just what you do," snorted Grandma. "But they never get the chance. They are scavengers. Opportunists. They eat what they can get. They have to."

"But … they don't do anything good, Grandma," I said.

Not like windsniffers, who keep the grubble population under control. Or gritterbacks, whose poop pats make the soil healthy.

"Don't do anything good?" Grandma snorted. "They don't do anything bad. And that's quite enough for me."

I looked at them. They *were* cute. And funny.

"Flo, we shall TAME these trolls," said Grandma.

"Is that a good idea, Grandma?" I said, feeling a bit doubtful.

"It is, Flo," said Grandma, pulling three jawjammers from her robe pocket, and feeding one to each baby.

"These are loyal little creatures. It takes a lot to gain their trust," Grandma said – just as all three babies tried to bite her fingers off – "but if you do, they will defend you to the death!"

"Grandma," I said. "How do you know so much about urban trolls?"

Grandma whipped a picture out of her robe pocket. A fully-grown urban troll – very ugly, and scowling at the camera – wearing a little collar. "Otto. Best pet I ever had," she said. Then wiped her eyes.

Grandma made a trail of food down the garden, most of it crunchy and spicy. "They'll sniff that out soon enough," she beamed.

Then she went back inside. Checked her potion. "Not much longer," she said, sprinkling in the disselslik. "Then my truth potion will be ready for the last – stinking – ingredients. And Ariadne will drink three drops, and be forced to CONFESS."

But I wondered. Grandma's plans – both of them, the troll taming *and* the truth potion – were they good plans? Or plans that were headed for total disaster?

Chapter 10

I was putting my pyjamas on when I heard the sound of a skyscooter. Hetty – back early, and *not* happy.

She burst into my room, grinding her teeth. "Jekyll…" she hissed. "He talked to me for *thirty seconds* at the Warts after-party. Then he got out a chart – a CHART! – of acceptable noses. He said he only dated witchgirls with a nose on the chart. And he *checked*, Flo, to see if my nose was on his chart. And it was NOT! So he stopped talking to me. And then – *then* – he spent all evening talking to a witchgirl whose nose WAS on the chart! Top of the chart! A big BIG nose, a three-bumper."

"Well – maybe he wasn't the right witchboy for you," I said. "Maybe you should find a witchboy who doesn't care about noses. Who cares about important things. A witchboy with more depth."

Hetty gaped. Then she glared. "Depth?" she hissed, right in my face. "I do NOT need depth in a witchboy! I need celebrity! And I also need a new *nose*! And a new *sister*!"

Then she marched out. And put on Shriek Sistaz – loud. But not loud enough to drown out the noise of a skycab coming in for a landing.

I heard the front door slam. And I could tell, just from the slam, that Mum was not happy either. Then I heard clattering sounds, and a shriek.

"Mother!" shrieked Mum. "How many times do I have to tell you? Do NOT leave your spare broomstick propped up in my HALLWAY!"

I stuck my head into the hallway, just as Mum's skychatter rang.

Next, Mum started shrieking into her skychatter. "Miranda. I *shall* do it! I SHALL!" she shrieked. "No, Miranda – I am NOT deluded … I know it's risky. I *know!* Yes, I *am* sorry for shrieking, Miranda, and I know I sound grumpy – but I *feel* grumpy. This is a business opportunity, and you are throwing cold water on it. COLD WATER! And *that*, Miranda, is why I feel grumpy!"

I had no idea what Mum was talking about but she swirled into the kitchen – then let out another shriek.

I ran in behind her. Mum was gaping down the back garden. At three small fluffy trolls guzzling their way up Grandma's food trail. And at two big – VERY big – not-at-all-fluffy trolls, also guzzling their way up the garden. Towards the back door. Fast.

"Can I not leave you alone for ONE MOMENT!" Mum shrieked at Grandma, who was busy stirring her cauldron.

Then Mum's fingers went flying over her spellstick. She marched to the back door, flung it open, and pointed her spellstick. "*Abrakkida Rune!*" she shrieked. "Get OUT of my garden!"

I had a good idea what spell Mum might be doing… An ejecting spell.

She was.

The mum troll, the dad, and two of the troll babies went flying through the air. Ejected – probably hundreds of miles – to land in some other witch's garden. Far far away.

But one troll baby escaped the spell and scuttled

off down the garden. Mum chased after it, pointing her spellstick. "I'll get you!" she shrieked. "I'll get you!"

She didn't.

The troll baby scuttled over the gate, and disappeared into the woods.

Then Mum swirled back up the path and in through the back door – just as Grandma dropped the last two ingredients into her potion.

First, the stinking idlewort.

Second, the reeking stenchflox.

✦

I canNOT describe the smell. I just can't. It was the sort of smell that there are NO WORDS to describe.

All I can say is this. The two stinks did *not* cancel each other out. They made each other worse. Clouds of fog – stinking sludgy brown fog – swirled round the kitchen. And me, Mum, Grandma – we all started to choke.

"WHAT ARE YOU DOING?" shrieked Mum, backing away, hands clapped to her mouth.

"Kristabel," spluttered Grandma, through her big hanky. "The stink will calm down. This is merely a first reaction. If we leave it, I have no doubt it will change."

And it DID change. It got stronger and stronger. Five – ten – times stronger. Then the potion started splittering and splattering out of the cauldron. So, choking and coughing, we all staggered out of the room. Then slammed the door shut.

"Mother!" hissed Mum, backed up against the door. "Get that potion OUT of my kitchen!"

Grandma drew herself up. "Certainly not, Kristabel. It is vital government work. It is a truth potion!"

Then she jabbed a finger at Mum. "I shall perfect my potion," said Grandma. "I shall reveal Ariadne Von Trinkpott for the thieving witchminister she is. And then, Kristabel – I shall go into business. Selling my truth potion."

"You will?" said Mum, sounding dangerous, which Mum sometimes does.

"Yes, Kristabel," said Grandma. "If you can be a businesswitch, so can I. And, Kristabel – I shall be a *better* businesswitch than you. Truth potion will turn me into the most successful Skritchett businesswitch in this family."

But Mum was already rushing off, making a noise – a sort of strangled *grrrrrr* – that only Grandma can get her to make.

It got worse.

At three o'clock in the morning the potion exploded. It sounded like a rocket going off, followed by huge thunderclaps. And potion – fizzing, fermenting, frothing potion – sprayed over every single bit of the kitchen…

And all that set off our security alarms. So two minutes later a witchwarden skyvan screeched up to the front door, and seven witchwardens tumbled out and surrounded the house. They started booming through loudhailers. Ordering the thieves to come out with their hands up.

"Enough," shrieked Mum. "ENOUGH!"

And at breakfast, Mum had an announcement. An announcement that Grandma was NOT happy about…

"A Shed, Kristabel?" said Grandma, glaring at Mum, and looking extremely grumpy. "You want me to live in a SHED?"

"Not a shed, Mother," said Mum wearily. "An *annexe*. Your own apartment. Your own place. A kitchen, sitting room, bedroom, bathroom. Everything. At the bottom of the garden."

"You want to get rid of me," snapped Grandma, glaring.

Mum shook her head. "I want to you to stay, Mother. Because I love you. But … well, I think it might be a little *easier* to love you if you are at the bottom of the garden, and I am at the top."

"I shall pack straight away," said Grandma huffily. "No need to build a shed, Kristabel. I shall live on the street. In the gutter."

I felt sorry for Mum. "Grandma," I said. "I think an annexe is a good idea. You can have it just how you want. With a frog flap, and a built-in broomstick holder, and everything."

Grandma glared at me. "You, Flo – now *you* want to get rid of me too."

Just then, Mum's skychatter rang and she bolted for her office. I heard her give a big shriek, then she started talking – very fast. A few minutes later, she came back into the kitchen, eyes glittering strangely.

"I have one more announcement," Mum said. "An … erm … exciting work opportunity has just been confirmed. I have to go away."

I wasn't surprised. Mum often goes away for work. "How long for?" I said.

"A while," said Mum – looking strangely shifty.

"A *while*?" Grandma said. "Kristabel, how long is a while?"

"I'm not sure," said Mum. "It depends."

That was odd. Usually Mum knows. And now

Mum was starting to look nervous. Which was also odd. Then I found out why.

"There is one more *teeny* thing," Mum said. "I think ... because I don't know quite how long I will be away ... because of the truth potion, the trolls, and so on ... it might be a good idea to get some kind of help here while I'm away."

"Help?" said Grandma, eyebrows knotting.

"Yes," said Mum, sounding even more nervous. "A live-in home help. A witch who will help things run smoothly."

Grandma was even crosser now. "A nanny, Kristabel?" she said. "You want me to have a nanny? You think I'm a silly old witch who might blow the house up? Or cause some ghastly injury to one of your daughters? Or get myself arrested, and leave them without an adult witch around?"

Mum was silent. Grandma had hit the nail on the head.

"So..." said Grandma, pulling herself up to her full height and glaring up at Mum. "One shed. One nanny. Are there more announcements, Kristabel? *More?*"

"No," said Mum, sighing. "That's the end of my announcements."

"Well, then," said Grandma, "I too have an

announcement. Which is this. I AM GOING TO MY ROOM."

Then Grandma stomped off, slamming the door behind her.

Chapter 11

Sunday got better after that because Lily and Kika came round.

"Clubbies," I told them. "That's what we're doing."

"Clubbies?" said Lily, looking suspicious. "What's that then?"

"A new fix-on," I said. "Mum got it for me."

I called up the first screen on my witchfixer and showed them.

WELCOME TO CLUBBIES!
EVERYTHING YOU NEED TO START A CLUB
WITH YOUR BESTIES!

Now, maybe by the time you read this book, lots of you witchkids will be using the Clubbies fix-on. But back then, it was brand new.

And now, in big flashing letters, the screen said this...

CLUBBIES – GETTING STARTED!

Welcome, club members. From now on you are all known as Clubbies!
Ready to start your very first meeting? Then get clicking!

CLUBBIE NAME!
CLUBBIE PASSWORD!
CLUBBIE HANDSHAKE!
CLUBBIE MOTTO!
CLUBBIE PROFILES!
CLOSING YOUR FIRST CLUBBIE MEETING!

Kika gasped and clasped her hands. "Flo, you are a GENIUS," she said. "This is the PERFECT thing to do today. Because this is an important day – the end of the holidays. And tomorrow, our last year as lower learners begins. Our last year in Charms. Our last year all together. Our—"

"Kika," said Lily. "Stop. Yes — Flo is going to a different upper school next year. But do you *have* to keep going on and ON about it?"

Because when we leave Charms and go to upper school, I'm going to Harridan's. Harridan College. Like Hetty. But I wish I wasn't. I'd rather go with Lily and Kika to Covens…

"Sorry, Flo," said Kika, patting my hand. "Lils is right. I have been *insensitive*. I have FAILED to think about how you might be feeling. I shall NOT mention this being our last year all together again. You have my *word*."

✦

We did the whole of Getting Started. First, we invented a name, then a Clubbie password — so no one, *especially* not Kika's little brothers, could get into Clubbies. And a secret seven-part Clubbie handshake, and a Clubbie motto.

Then we filled in the Clubbie profiles…

CLUBBIE PROFILES

Load a cool pic of each Clubbie!
Click here to create pic box!

Now fill in the Clubbie info underneath!

ALL ABOUT YOU!

Name
Address
Birth date
Eye colour
Hair colour
Best feature
Robe size
Shoe size
First memory
Best day ever

MORE ABOUT YOU!

Fave activity
Fave celeb
Fave takeaway
Fave drink
Fave colour
Fave animal – magical
Fave animal – non-magical
Fave witchscreen show
Fave band
Fave holiday

Me and Lily sat there gaping at Kika's answers.

"Kika," said Lily. "Your best feature – is it really your toes? *Really?*"

Kika beamed. "It is, Lils," she said proudly. "I have beautiful toes."

"And your first memory," I said. "Seeing the ghost of a unicorn cantering through your garden... Kika, are you *sure* that's an actual memory? Not a dream?"

"Yes," said Kika. "I definitely saw it. It was there. Definitely."

Then she looked thrilled. "This is a *good* thing we are doing – Clubbies," she said. "A fun thing. And it is helping us build a strong bond of friendship. Because it is important not to take friendships for granted. Important to look after your friendships. And—"

Lily clapped a hand over Kika's mouth, and I sat on her. Then we did the last screen...

CLOSING YOUR FIRST CLUBBIE MEETING!

Congratulations, Clubbies! Your club is now OPEN!
So make it official – take a pic of all Clubbie members!

Upload it to the certificate, then print it out and all sign it!

This is to certify that we have, as of today (date)....................... become Clubbies.

Click here to create Clubbie pic box!

The name of our club is...........................

And we hereby all sign our names below:

ALL DONE? THEN CLICK HERE TO ORDER YOUR FREE CLUBBIE BADGES AND BINDER!

WARNING!!!! THUNDERBOLT DELIVERY!!!!

So Lily got her skychatter out. "Clubbies," she said. "POSE!"

And we got a picture of all three of us. Grinning and giving a thumbs-up. We uploaded it, printed out the certificate and all signed it.

Then we clicked...

It took less than one minute. Then a huge clap of thunder shook the garden. My window flew open –

and a parcel shot in and landed on my bed.

It had a big label on it.

WHIRLYGIRLS CLUB

Inside the parcel were three shiny badges that said Whirlygirls Club. A big green binder – with a padlock that only the Clubbie code would open. And a label on it...

TOP SECRET! FOR CLUBBIE EYES ONLY!!!

Then another screen came up on the witchfixer...

COMING UP! MORE MEETINGS!
Secret stuff! School stuff! Sleepover stuff!
Spooky stuff!
Holiday stuff! Picnic stuff! Party stuff!
Camping stuff!

And much MUCH more!!!!
AND ONE LAST THING!
Any time you want to add a new Clubbie member, click here!

"Well, we won't need *that*," I said, closing Clubbies. "There will be NO new members. Just us."

But closing Clubbies took my witchfixer straight back to the witchweb, straight to the *Haggnews* screen – and the *Haggnews* headlines…

Kika gasped. "Flo, look!" she said.

And there I was. Headline news again.

With a picture, caught on spycam. Me clinging to the top of the Haggfiend statue. And a headline…

FEARLESS FLO IN
REAL-LIFE
HAGGFIEND HORROR!

It was all there. Not just the story of that day, of the windwhirl and us ending up on the Haggfiend statue – but the whole story. *My* whole story. Of Dad being missing, of the ghoul attack. Everything.

Kika was thrilled. "Flo," she said. "You are NEWS! Again!"

Then she grabbed my arm and wagged a finger in my face. "You wasted the opportunity to be a celebrity last time," she said sternly. "But now, Flo – *now* – witchpaps will be back! You have a second chance!"

"I don't *want* a second chance," I said.

But now Kika was gasping again. "Look! Look!" she said. "Flo is not the only witchgirl with a headline in Haggspit!"

So me and Lily looked...

POTIONS MOGUL TAKES IN
EXTRA ORPHAN!

Some orphan – abandoned at birth, living on the streets – had been discovered sheltering from the windwhirls in a garden shed at the Hurlstruk Happy Home.

And Mr Potions2Go listened to her tale. Then decided she should join all the other, smaller orphans, and live in his new Hurlstruk Happy Home.

Kika could NOT stop clasping her hands together. "An orphan!" she gasped. "Plucked from the gutter by a mogul!"

Lily wasn't happy about my headline. "Me and you were Fearless too," she grumbled to Kika. "Why is it just Fearless *Flo*?"

"No, Lily," said Kika, shaking her head, eyes popping. "I absolutely wasn't Fearless." Then she gave a sigh. "Fearlessness is simply not a good point that I have identified in myself."

"Well, *I* was Fearless," said Lily, scowling at me now.

Now Kika wagged her finger in Lily's face. "Lils," she said. "Stop that. You were *not* Fearless like Flo was."

But Lily sat there, still glaring, still scowling. So Kika pointed at Lily's robes, then mine, then hers. "What are these, Lils?" she said sternly.

"Clubbie badges," Lily mumbled.

"And *why* are we wearing Clubbie badges, Lils?" said Kika, even more sternly.

"Because we're best friends," Lily mumbled. "Witchbesties forever."

Then she looked a bit sheepish. "Sorry, Flo," she said. "I know you can't help being headlines."

"Maybe something else will happen," said Kika, looking hopeful. "Prongles stampeding through our school playground like they just did in Drakken. And us three can head the prongles off – and ALL be headlines."

"I hope not," I said. "I want NO MORE headlines. Nothing strange or scary to happen. Not ever again."

And I meant it.

I wanted to be just me. Florence Skritchett, extremely ordinary witchkid.

Yes, that's what I wanted – and THAT, I thought, was how it would be.

But I was wrong. *Very* wrong.

Part
Two

Chapter 12

"Darling," said Mum, swooshing into the kitchen where I was eating breakfast. "It is NOT too late to change your mind. The skyshredder is ready. Ready to go. This *minute* – this very minute."

"Mum," I said, finishing my shivershake and putting my glass in the witchwasher. "I don't want to change my mind. I want to take the skybus. I have never EVER taken the skybus to school."

I have been going to Charms since I was four. But up to now, Mum has always dropped me off in the skyshredder.

"But, darling," Mum said, and I could see she was

really panicking, "only ordinary witchchildren take the skybus. *Ordinary* witchchildren."

"Yes," I said. "Which is why I want to take it. I AM an ordinary witchchild."

Mum slumped. "Why, darling? Why? Hetty *never* took the skybus. Never."

"No way," said Hetty, staggering in, yawning, still half asleep. "Get up ten minutes early? Just to get a skybus? When I can arrive in style? Not a chance. But then you…" she said, flicking my ear, "have always been weird – and we all know why."

Yes. The Accident. Being dropped on my head by a skragglehead when I was almost two. That's what made me like I am – according to Hetty.

Now Mum was chewing her lip. "But, darling … suppose something happens? Suppose there are *thieves* waiting in the skybus shelter? Suppose they steal your backpack. Or your skychatter? Or your kidcard?"

"Mum," I said, putting my backpack on. "I am meeting Kika on the corner, and Lily on the skybus. I am not on my own."

Because Lily and Kika consulted the Book when I said we should get the skybus. And it said this, on page 86 – *Facing new challenges…* "Growing up is an exciting time. A time to be bold! Be brave! Seize new challenges! New opportunities!"

So the Book did something useful for once.

Mum grabbed my arm. "Look both ways, crossing the Bouncing Bridge. *Both* ways!" she said.

"Mum," I said. "STOP worrying. I can look after myself."

But now Mum grabbed me by both shoulders. "Darling," she said. "Here are the rules. No talking to ordinary witchchildren. No talking to grown-up witches. No accepting jawjammers from strangers. No patting unknown boggles. And no—"

"Bye, Mum," I said, shrugging her off. Then I gave her a kiss. And set off. Fast.

✦

Kika was on the corner, hopping from foot to foot, looking extremely proud, but biting her lip.

"Flo," she said, as we walked to the skybus stop. "This is a VERY big day. The start of our last year in Charms. And it is *fitting* that on this very big day, we are taking this very big step. Taking the skybus alone."

Then she grabbed my arm. Looked at me earnestly. "But, Flo," she said, "this new challenge we are facing, this opportunity we are seizing – we may find we feel nervous. Scared even. This is quite natural and nothing for us to worry about."

By the time Kika stopped talking, we were at the skybus stop – and a green and red speck appeared in the distance. Skybus 401, a double-decker.

It landed, and the doors hissed open. I pressed my kidcard down on the reader. It pinged and I went up the stairs, Kika following.

The top deck was full of witchkids. Noisy witchkids.

Me and Kika found a window seat. Opposite, two witchteens sat listening to something – one earphone each – and waggling their heads.

Two stops later, Lily came up the stairs and joined us – just as the two witchteens stopped waggling, took the earphones out and started staring at me.

"You…"said one of them, leaning forward. "You're Fearless Flo! The Haggfiend Horror witchkid. You were up there." She pointed back up the mountain. At the Haggfiend statue, towering above us. "On its nose."

"She was," said Kika, beaming proudly.

"So – what was it like?" said the other witchteen. "Actually being up there? Was it *totally* terrifying?"

Both witchteens were staring at me. And now other witchkids on the skybus were staring too.

I felt myself go bright green. I stared down at my own shoes. "Erm…" I said.

Then Lily barged in. "I can tell you exactly what it was like," she said. "Because I am *also* a fearless survivor of Haggfiend Horror. I was also on the statue. On its shoulder."

"Yeah," said one of the witchteens, making an unimpressed sort of face. "But you're not Fearless *Flo*, are you? I mean, this is her second time of being headlines. Fearless Flo and the Ghouls, and now Fearless Flo and Haggfiend Horror."

"And, Josie –" said the other witchteen, butting in, "she was also Tragic Flo. Because of the Dad thing."

Which I was. All the headlines called me Tragic Flo when Dad went missing.

Then the Josie one looked at me. "It's like you're *destined* to be famous!" she said. "Like it's fate!"

And now both of them stood up to get off, looking at me as if I was some kind of actual celebrity. As for Lily – she was glaring again. Not happy.

"Lils," Kika said sternly, as we got off the skybus. "Remember. Just as you said – it is totally NOT Flo's fault that she keeps being headlines. Celebrity just seeks her out."

Then Kika gasped. "Look!" she said. "Look!"

So I did.

There were witchpaps. Lots of them. Outside the school gates.

Kika grabbed my arm. "Pose, Flo, pose. This is your big moment!"

But it *wasn't* my big moment. Because the witchpaps were NOT interested in me. They were interested in something else.

In a skyswaggerer – twelve-seater at least – swooping in for a landing.

Chapter 13

A witchgirl was bundled out of the skyswaggerer and in through the school gates by two witches. Ms Riggle, our headteacher, came rushing out to meet them, and the witchpaps went crazy. Clicking. Shouting. Witchpappers flashing.

And whoever she was – we only got a glimpse of her before she was rushed inside. But all around me, I could hear the playground buzzing with talk.

Witchgirls gasping and chattering…

"Who is she? Who IS she?"

"A celebrity. In our school! *Ours*. It is like a DREAM COME TRUE!"

"She might be in our class. Our *actual* class!"

"We might be friends. Friends with a celebrity!"

"Which makes us – US! – practically celebrities!"

And the witchboys were just as bad...

"So ... what class is that celebrity going to be in?"

"Hard to say. She was a skinny sort of celebrity. Short. Olive Class, I reckon."

"Not Olive. She was not *that* short. She was skinny, I'll give you that – but she was short*ish*. NOT short. She'll be in Avocado Class."

"What's she a celebrity for, then? Gripball? Did she have gripball legs?"

"No WAY. Not gripball legs. Spindly legs, she had – might be more of a bikkelbat player."

On and on and on.

Luckily just then Mr Prankett came swooshing down the steps and over to our line.

"Emerald Class," he said, pointing his spellstick and showering us all with confetti. "The new year begins!"

★

Emerald Class was full of witchkids I have known for years, but this year our classroom was right at the top of the school building.

We trooped inside behind Mr Prankett. Looked

around. At the walls, empty for now. At the tables laid out in long straight rows, because the government says rows are how witchkids learn best.

Mr Prankett was shaking his head. "No, no, no. No rows," he said. Then his fingers went flying, he pointed his spellstick – and all the tables shot off the ground, and up into the air. They whizzed around, rearranging themselves, then plonked themselves down – in groups of four.

"Better," said Mr Prankett. Then he looked round and gave an evil cackle. "And now, Emerald Class," he said, "it is *your* turn."

Then he pointed his spellstick again.

I felt odd, I felt strange – and most of all my feet felt itchy. And I knew what was about to happen. Because Grandma has done this to me before…

It *did* happen.

I shot off the floor, up in the air and across the room. Along with Lily and Kika, and the whole of Emerald Class.

And, for the first time EVER, me and Lily and Kika found ourselves sitting at a table together.

We beamed. And all around us, other witchkids were beaming.

But not Mamie Swip. Mamie was NOT beaming,

and then her hand shot up.

"Mr Prankett," she said, sternly. "Are you aware that was actually *illegal*?"

Mamie's mum works for the government. She's Education Witchminister, and Grandma met her once in Argument House. "Takes herself FAR too seriously," she said. "No jokes. EVER."

Mamie is just like her.

"Mamie," Mr Prankett said. "I am simply following instructions." He waved a big document that said this on the cover...

MANUAL OF BEST PRACTICE

"This manual is from the Education Department," said Mr Prankett. "Signed by *your mother*, Mamie. It tells me how to teach. And it says here: *To maximise contact teaching time, witchteachers must ensure witchchildren are seated as quickly as possible at the start of the day.*"

Then he beamed at Mamie. Who looked a bit confused.

"Now, Emerald Class," Mr Prankett said. "The timetable." And sheets of paper came winging across the classroom and landed on every desk.

"You will see from your timetable that our first

lesson is witchglobe studies," said Mr Prankett. "And first – the Class Directive."

The Class Directive…

We all groaned.

Here in United Witchenlands Class Directives are issued by the government at the start of each year. Guides for the witchteacher about what witchkids should learn in each subject. And Class Directives are hardly ever good news.

"This year in witchglobe studies," said Mr Prankett, "Emerald Class will do one global study and one local study. The global study will be of the Narrowlands."

I crossed my fingers. I wanted to learn about the early witchsettlers in the Narrowlands. Because that's interesting – how they arrived and thought they were the first witches there, but they weren't. How tiny scattered tribes – heckles – of witches were already there. How many attacks, and ambushes, and big magic battles they had – settlers against heckles. How the heckles lost in the end. Got rounded up, and stuck in the worst bit of the Narrowlands – which is now Gurrk.

But no. The global study of the Narrowlands was about dragon-oil production in Golmenn.

By the time Mr Prankett had read us all that,

Mervikk – Mervikk Ashbok – was jiggling and fidgeting…

Mervikk is my friend. He speaks three languages. Witchen, obviously. But also Flungtung and Grimmish.

His mum's from Biktek – the mountainous Farflung – and his dad's from Bittergrim in the Grimlands. And Mervikk has taught me counting, up to ten, in Flungtung and Grimmish. He has also taught me three words in Grimmish and two in Flungtung that a witchkid is *not* supposed to know.

But Mervikk canNOT sit still. He finds it too hard. And Mr Prankett knows that, because Mervikk is in his extra class after school.

Mr Prankett also knows the best way to stop Mervikk jiggling and fidgeting. "Mervikk," he said. "You have thirty seconds. Go!"

So Mervikk shot out of his seat and ran – no, galloped – round the room, flapping his arms and jumping as he went.

"Mervikk," said Mr Prankett. "Stop!"

And Mervikk shot back into his seat.

"And now – our local study," said Mr Prankett. "The impact of tourism on Haggspit."

We all groaned. And Mervikk started to pretend he was being sick.

Mr Prankett held up his hand – and straight away we all stopped groaning, and Mervikk sat bolt upright. Because you don't actually mess with Mr Prankett.

"Our first lesson," Mr Prankett said, "will be to read this." Then he waved a book at us:

Magical Myths of the Witchenlands.

The whole class started beaming again. Because having a story read to us – especially by Mr Prankett who does all the voices and actions – was a good start to lessons.

But once again, Mamie was NOT beaming. Her eyebrows shot up, and so did her hand.

"Mr Prankett," she said, and she was shaking her head so hard she looked like a windsniffer trying to dry itself after a wallow in the river. "We are not *allowed* exciting books, or funny books, because they might affect class discipline. And we are not allowed scary books, because they might give us nightmares. And THAT book is all three."

"Mamie," said Mr Prankett. "All witchchildren should have nightmares. Nightmares exercise a witchchild's lungs."

Which is the sort of the thing Dad would say. The sort of thing that makes me laugh. But Mamie just looked even more confused.

"Besides, Mamie," Mr Prankett said, looking very serious, "it is *vital* we read this book. The Haggfiend myth is a huge part of tourism in Haggspit."

Which is true. All summer long there are witchtourists in Haggspit buying Haggfiend key rings and tea towels, Haggfiend sunhats and spellstick holders, and taking tours up to the Haggfiend statue.

"These stories started off as tales told at night by firelight," Mr Prankett said. Then he pointed his spellstick, and the room went darker. And, in front of his desk, on the classroom floor, the flickering green flames of a fire lit up the room.

Mamie half stuck her hand in the air, and then put it down again.

Mr Prankett spotted her. "Mamie," he said. "It says here: *Magicreations or magimirages are permissible if they contribute to students' understanding of the subject.*"

He leaned forward. "Imagine these stories," he said, "handed down from one generation of cave witches to the next. The witchchildren, huddled in the cave in their fur robes, sitting round the fire, listening, as the story is told. And those cave witchchildren, in turn, telling the story to their young."

Mr Prankett opened the book. "These myths we read now," he said, "are the final version of those tales, handed down by the fireside."

Then Mr Prankett opened up *Magical Myths*, and began to read. The story I knew so well…

Chapter 14

"Haggfiend Horror"

Witchchildren, our terrible story – our terrible tale – begins with the tribe of the Haggs. Wild witches, fierce sorceresses, with long stringy hair, and cruel magic ways.

Witches would shiver, witches would quake, when they heard the screech of the Haggs flying by. For witches feared the Haggs – just as you, witchchildren, may fear the dark and the night.

But the Haggs themselves were full of fear – fear of their very own queen. Queen Aggrakkala, the most terrible of all the terrible Haggs.

"Bring me the head of an old Hagg, a useless Hagg – for I am peckish," Queen Aggrakkala would snarl at her servants. "And be quick about it!"

Terror struck at the heart of every Hagg. Terror … and fury. "Sisters," they said, meeting in secret. "We must get rid of her. Before she gets rid of all of US!"

And the Haggs did.

Under cover of darkness they struck and strapped their ghastly queen to a serpent that roamed the bay.

How the poor beast struggled. How it raged. How it tried to shed itself of its ghastly load, churning the seas so high the waves swamped the land.

But the Haggs stood high up on the clifftops, shooting down arrows of fire – and at last, with a howl, the wretched beast surged out to sea.

Three days and three nights the

serpent swam the vast seas. Then, in a wild and mountainous place, it landed. And the Hagg broke free.

"I must be fed," she screamed – but no servants came.

And so the starving Hagg raged and roamed. Roamed far and wide, between a mountain that moaned and a stillwater that sang.

And there, in a cave, close by the stillwater – she made her lair.

Then one day, as she roamed, the Hagg found a nest, filled with squiggling grey worms. She scooped them up. "Deliciously squishy," she said, smacking her lips.

She heard a growl behind her. The growl of a huge hairy Fiend. "Leave this place," he roared, baring his teeth. "For I am starving. I will feast on those fine squiggling worms!"

"I will NOT leave," the Hagg snarled. "For I was once Queen of the Haggs! And these worms are my feast."

"I was once King of the Fiends," he snarled back. "So do as I say!"

For indeed he was once King, and he too was banished – just as was the Hagg.

Then the two starving creatures began to fight. The strength of the Fiend against the cunning of the Hagg.

For seven days and seven nights the battle raged. Then, at last...

"A draw," gasped the Hagg.

"A draw," gasped the Fiend.

So together they feasted on the squiggling grey worms and the two ghastly creatures fell in love.

Then, one stormy night, in the wilds of winter – as thunder roared and lightning cracked – a baby was born of their union...

The Haggfiend.

$\star$

"She is a BEAUTY," said the Hagg. "A face of such astonishing evil. A screech to strike terror into witches' hearts. Just like her mummy."

"And such power in her hairy haunches," said the Fiend. "Such fine hooves, cloven and huge. Such a fine poison barb on her tail. Just like her daddy."

For, witchchildren – THIS was the Haggfiend. Head and arms of Hagg, body of Fiend.

Year by year the ghastly Haggfiend grew. A vicious snarling creature, with hair that lived and eyes that flamed. Flowers wilted where she walked. All creatures, all witches, were rendered senseless and still by one look at her terrible face, by one smell of her terrible smell.

And not one kind thought in her head did she have. Not one kind word for her mother or father. By day and by night, she bossed them both.

"Fetch my slippers," she would snarl. "For I NEVER asked to be brought into this world – and my hooves are cold."

By day and by night, the two wretched parents scurried to do her bidding.

And, as the Haggfiend grew, so did her ghastly powers. She wielded a wand of terrible power and strength. Day by day her dark enchantments grew.

She had magic in her fingernails, in her eyes, in her hooves – and nothing but evil in her cold cruel heart.

So ghastly was the Haggfiend that – when she was but fifteen years old – she summoned her mother and her father to the Kraggs of Kroke. "You are old and useless," she snarled. "You fetch my slippers too slowly. You catch too few worms for my supper."

For those squiggling grey worms were the favourite feast of the Haggfiend.

Then she pushed first her father, then her mother, off the Kraggs. And with a scream, they were gone. Dashed to pieces on the rocks of the Roaring Rapids below.

And, the very next day...

"I must have servants," screamed the Haggfiend. "Witchgirls to feed me, to comb my hair, to stir my potions, to polish my strong hooves, to clean out my lair."

Witchchildren, if you tremble too

easily – NOW is the time to stop reading.

For the Haggfiend gathered around her flying humped creatures, mild of manner and simple of brain – and bewitched by one stare from the Haggfiend's eyes.

Then, together with her creatures, she roamed the hills, roamed the forests around her, found a small witchgirl, walking alone.

"Seize her," she commanded her flying humped creatures. "Bring her to my lair. She shall be my servant. Do my bidding, day and night."

So that terrified witchgirl swept and cleaned, she polished and cooked. Until, one day, she hurried to the Haggfiend, a dish of squiggling grey worms in her hands. But alas, in her haste, the dish fell from her hands, and was smashed to pieces by the Haggfiend's huge hooves.

The fury of the Haggfiend was fearsome to see. "She displeases me!" she raged to her flying humped creatures. "She works too slowly! One servant is not enough for the glorious Haggfiend! Find me others! Less clumsy!"

So that one poor witchgirl was the first – but not the last. One after another, witchgirls were snatched. Flown to the lair to do the Haggfiend's bidding.

Yet never was the Haggfiend satisfied. "She stirs my potion with the wrong spoon!" the Haggfiend would rage. "She tugs too hard on my hair with the comb! She leaves dust in the corners of my glorious lair! Fetch me more witchgirls. More servants! Better ones!"

★

Soon witches marched to the great palace of the Hovelhaggs. "Stop this ghastly creature from stealing our witchgirls, we beg you," they urged their rulers.

But the Esteemed Graciouswitches did nothing. "This Haggfiend – she plucks only poor witchgirls from the forest," they said to each other. "Why should we care?"

Until, one night, the Haggfiend came to the palace, disguised as a poor beggarwitch.

For the Haggfiend was cruel, she was clever, she was cunning – and she had one terrible gift...

The gift of disguise. Disguise as a witch of any kind. One thing only revealed who she really was – her feet had no toes. For the one thing the Haggfiend could not fully disguise was her hooves.

Dressed in tatters, her feet bound in rags to hide the terrible truth – she knocked at the gates of the palace.

"Spare a brikkel for a poor witch left in unfortunate circumstances," she quavered. "For I am starving."

"Be gone," said Queen Hinkel, ruler of the Hovelhaggs. "Be off with you."

But so busy was Queen Hinkel at the gates that she knew not what had happened behind her. In a courtyard of the great palace, the flying humped creatures had snatched a small Graciouswitch at play with her brothers and sister.

✦

Now - at last - the Esteemed Graciouswitches were ready to act. "She has stolen our precious daughter. Who will rid us of this ghastly Haggfiend?" roared Queen Hinkel. "Any witch who can do so will have one chest of gold from our coffers!"

And so a proclamation was sent out throughout the Witchenlands.

A poor witchgirl heard it. Ran home to her grandmother - one old in years, but wise in the ways of all witches.

"Grandmother, what shall I do?" said the witchgirl. "How shall I rid our land of the hideous Haggfiend?"

"Child," said the grandmother. "You are too precious. It is too dangerous."

"Grandmother," said the witchgirl. "I shall go anyway. But if you help me - then maybe I shall return."

"Go to my potion cupboard," said the grandmother. "Bring me the small silver bottle with the jewelled green stopper."

The grandmother held up the bottle. "This bottle holds a potion of strong and dangerous enchantment," she said. "Not strong enough to rid us of the Haggfiend forever, yet strong enough to plunge her deep into an enchanted sleep. You must seek out your chance to use it."

And so the brave little witchgirl went skipping through the forest. Day after day she skipped – until the day came...

"There!" screeched the Haggfiend. "That small dancing witchgirl. She shall be my new servant!"

And so the flying humped creatures carried her off to the Haggfiend's lair.

★

Trapped in the Haggfiend's lair – in the dark, in the damp, with those hundreds of witchgirls – the witchgirl huddled. She shivered. She quaked.

And, in the middle of the lair, a

cauldron of vast size bubbled and steamed.

"Now!" shrieked the Haggfiend, stamping her huge hooves, swishing her long tail. "Newest of my servants – climb the ladder to my cauldron! Take the wooden spoon that hangs on the hook! And STIR my potion three times!"

And so the brave witchgirl climbed and climbed.

"This potion shall keep me the beauty I am FOREVER!" the Haggfiend screeched. "One cup each day from now on!"

Trembling, terrified, the witchgirl stirred. Once, twice, three times – as the Haggfiend paced her lair.

Then – as the Haggfiend's huge back was turned away – she took the stopper from the small silver potion bottle. And she poured...

"Is it done?" screeched the Haggfiend, turning and pacing towards her. "Is it DONE?"

"It is done," said the witchgirl. Then

she scooped out a cupful - and the Haggfiend drank.

✦

She knew. From the very first sip, that hideous Haggfiend knew.

"My fingernails tingle! You have TRICKED me," she shrieked. "This potion is not mine! This potion will NOT do what I wish!"

She stretched out her ghastly hands. "I shall—"

Then the Haggfiend began to yawn.

"Are you sleepy, dear Haggfiend?" said the small, brave witchgirl. "Shall I fetch you a soft pillow?"

And the Haggfiend yawned again.

But, witchchildren, as her eyes closed, as her breathing grew slow, as she lay down in her lair, the Haggfiend spoke. Spoke these, her very last words...

"One day, little witchgirl," she hissed. "One day I will awaken. And then, I shall have my REVENGE!"

Then she fell - deep, DEEP - into enchanted sleep. And there she lies still, never ageing one day. Never to awake, as long as she sleeps undisturbed in her lair.

But fear not, witchchildren. No witch would EVER move the Haggfiend from her lair. No witch would EVER disturb her from her enchanted sleep.

For all witches know - if the Haggfiend should wake, no witchgirl is safe. Not anywhere.

Chapter 15

Just as Mr Prankett finished reading, the classroom door opened. And in walked Ms Riggle.

"Emerald Class," she said. "You have a new classmate."

And a witchgirl walked in behind her. A witchgirl I recognised...

The runaway. The orphan. The headline news.

Ferocity. That was her name.

She had a thin face, a pointy nose, a high swishy ponytail – and every witchkid in Emerald Class was goggling at her, and whispering. Witchkids who knew who Ferocity was, whispering information to witchkids who didn't.

Mr Prankett noticed the goggling, the whispering. He looked round. "Emerald Class," he said. "I see many of you know who Ferocity is." Then he looked serious. "So you will also know that Ferocity has not had an easy start in life."

Ferocity looked at the floor, mouth turned down.

"But now Ferocity has a new beginning," said Mr Prankett. "And it is up to us to help Ferocity with her new beginning. To make her feel welcome."

Then Mamie Swip's hand shot up. "Mr Prankett," she said. "I suggest that I am in charge of helping Ferocity with her new beginning. With making her feel welcome."

"Thank you, Mamie," said Mr Prankett. "But I already have someone in mind." Which was when I realised — there was only one empty seat in the room. At our table.

"Flo," said Mr Prankett. "You will help Ferocity. Look after her. Answer her questions."

Straight away Lily butted in. "Mr Prankett. *I* can do helping too. And looking after. And answering questions. Me *and* Flo."

Then Kika's hand shot up. "Me too, Mr Prankett," she said, nodding. "You can rely on me to help

Ferocity with her new beginning. Because Ferocity may be feeling shy and nervous. And if she is, I can help her. Not just Flo. Also me. And Lily. Ferocity can rely on us."

Then Kika ran out of breath.

And as soon as the screecher went off for breaktime, Lily grabbed one of Ferocity's arms and Kika grabbed the other. Then they whisked her out to the playground and started firing questions at her.

"So … Hurlstruk Happy Home," said Lily. "What's it like?"

"Is it big? Is it comfy? Does it feel like a dream come true?" said Kika, clasping her hands together.

Ferocity clasped *her* hands together. Looked round – because all the witchgirls in my class were gathered round now, wanting to hear her answers. Then Ferocity spoke.

"It *does* feel like a dream come true," she said, eyes shining. "I have my own room. It's warm. Clean. Comfortable. And the grown-ups are kind."

Then her voice started to wobble. "It's not been easy," she said. "Having no family. Not knowing who I am. Where I came from."

Then she sniffed. "Just dumped, in a little basket, outside the witchwarden station. No name. No label. Nothing."

Ferocity looked round sadly. "I don't even know when my birthday is," she said. "Never celebrated it."

Every witchgirl in Emerald Class gasped.

"But … that means you have NEVER had a birthday cake!" gasped Mamie. "Never."

She looked round. "Emerald Class," she said. "We must make a birthday cake. Ferocity, choose a birthday – any day – and we'll BAKE!"

And every witchgirl started nodding.

"So…" Lily said, "what happened to you after the little basket?"

"I was put in an orphanage," Ferocity said. She gave a big shiver. "Not a lovely one like Hurlstruk Happy Home. A horrible one. One with *cruel* grown-ups. Grown-ups who put witchchildren in DARK CUPBOARDS full of spiders. Just for sweeping the floors too slowly."

The witchboys had stopped playing gripball now. They started crowding round, listening.

"I was about four when I ran away," Ferocity said. "Packed a tiny bag with my only possessions – a few rags of clothes, the rough blanket from my bed. Then I stowed away in a skytruck. Hid in a crate of glimberries. And that was it. I was on the streets."

She paused. Looked round. Every witchkid in Emerald Class was listening now. Goggling at Ferocity. She gave a shiver. "But that very first night on the streets," she said, "I woke under my rough blanket and saw EYES staring at me."

"Eyes? What sort of eyes?" gasped Kika.

"Big yellow eyes," said Ferocity. "Strimmershank eyes! A three-horned strimmershank. Snarling, and ready to pounce!"

"What did you do? What did you DO?" Kika gasped.

"I jabbed it in the eyes," said Ferocity. "Hard as I could. Then – I ran!"

Now, a thought popped into my head at that moment. Ferocity's story, the way she was telling it…

It reminded me of something.

And that something was called Plucky – a forest pixie I met with Grandma.

Plucky was in the Sanctuary, a specially made home for the pixies, where they're all kept safe. Because the pixies have no forest right now. Not since it all burned down.

Only Plucky turned out NOT to be a forest pixie. He turned out to be a doppel, a shapeshifting maggot. The sort of maggot that shapeshifts and joins a herd – goblins, grinthogs, dragons, a doppel doesn't care – then pretends to be sick so the herd looks after it.

So Plucky, the doppel, shapeshifted into a forest pixie. And I watched him on the witchweb – because the pixies are filmed in the Sanctuary twenty-four hours a day – telling the other forest pixies his story. And I don't speak Pixish, but it was clear Plucky was telling the pixies a tragic story. About losing all his family. About his terrible journey to get to the Sanctuary…

The forest pixies fell for it. They all stood around, gasping and sobbing as they listened to the pack of lies Plucky was telling them.

And now, standing here in the playground, listening to Ferocity's story – I could NOT stop thinking of Plucky.

By now every witchkid in Emerald Class was goggling more. Some were tearful and dabbing at their eyes. Including Lily and Kika.

"So…" said Lily, looking really upset. "How did you learn to *read*? To *write*?"

Ferocity sniffed. Her lip wobbled. "Had to teach myself," she said. "There was a witch who was kind to me. In the library."

She dabbed her eyes. "Not many witches were kind to a homeless orphan," she said. "But she let me hide in a corner of the library and read."

"And…" said Henka Sprigg, in a hushed voice, "you were almost a STARVING orphan too."

Ferocity nodded. "I used to catch gutter nibbets, eat them raw," she said, with a shiver, as every witchkid gasped. "I hope I *never* have to eat another one."

Then she looked round, eyes huge. "There was just one lucky time," she said, "I had FRIED gutter nibbets! A witchtramp – all wrinkly, with big black gaps instead of teeth – was frying some up on a little fire. And he let me have some."

She smacked her lips. "They were SO good. I can taste them now," she said. "Like a banquet!"

"So what's it taste like?" said Lily. "Fried gutter nibbet?"

"Very … nibbety," Ferocity said. "Spicy and crunchy."

Now – I know about fried gutter nibbets. Because Dad ate some for his work. Dad was a witchscreen presenter, and one show he did was called *Stuff*. And on *Stuff*, he had to eat fried gutter nibbets. He said they tasted of nothing, and they were very chewy and stringy…

So why did Ferocity say they were spicy and crunchy?

And that's when the thought popped into my head... Perhaps because she had never actually tasted fried gutter nibbets.

Then the screecher went for the end of breaktime, and we all went inside.

"Rags to riches," Kika said, clasping her hands as we climbed the stairs. "It's a rags to riches story. Like a fairytale!"

And I couldn't help thinking that, yes. It was.

It was *just* like a fairytale...

Chapter 16

A witch was coming out of our front gate as I walked up the road home from school.

I got just a glimpse of her. A neat, tidy-looking witch. Neat, tidy robes, and neat, tidy hair – and big clumpy shoes on her feet.

Mum was standing in the hallway, looking pleased, as I came in. "Flo," she said, "we have a new home help starting on Wednesday. Her name is Malinka. You will like her, I am sure."

Mum frowned. "Although it is strangely puzzling," she said. "I expected a *queue* of witches to interview for the job. But there was only Malinka. Not one other witch. None at all. Most unexpected."

Then – as usual – Mum's skychatter rang. She looked at the number. "Flo," she said, eyes glittering, "this is a call I must take in *private*! A vital work call!"

She swirled across the hallway and into her office, then shut the door firmly behind her.

I could hear Grandma in the sitting room, chatting to someone. So I stuck my head round the door. Grandma was hunched in front of her magic mirror, another old witch hunched beside her.

Auntie Mims…

Mimosa Jaggwort – Lily's great-auntie, who lives in Lily's house and is also Grandma's friend.

Grandma and Auntie Mims were both staring at the magic mirror.

The magic mirror takes up one whole wall of the sitting room, and right now it was set to Roaming. Showing lots of small pictures of Haggspit. Constantly changing pictures – of the harbour, the town, the mountains, the buildings.

"Mimosa," Grandma was saying, "we must keep our eyes peeled. That witch Ariadne Von Trinkpott is cheating our government – and I am now compiling a DOSSIER!"

"A dossier?" quavered Auntie Mims, which is how Auntie Mims speaks.

"I am keeping notes, Mimosa," said Grandma. "Notes on that witch's cheating activities. Times, dates and pictures."

Then she opened her notepad. "Last Wednesday," she said. "Subject sighted. Twelve forty-seven. Dining at Yumyums."

"Yumyums?" quavered Auntie Mims.

"FOUR courses, Mimosa," said Grandma. "She claimed it was a working lunch – got the government to pay for it – when it was *nothing* of the sort. It was not a working lunch, it was a fun lunch. A meal with three friends. Bridesmaids at her wedding – her *fifth* wedding, Mimosa – last year.

"And this…" Grandma said, waving a picture. "See this? *Proof!*"

There were four witches in the picture, looking like they were having a very good time.

"Taken by a professional, Mimosa," said Grandma proudly. "Edikk Storkkensnap. Edikk is part of my team, taking ALL the pictures for my Dossier."

Edikk Storkkensnap…

I had a feeling I knew who Edikk was. The most annoying witchpap of all. The one who kept shouting through the letterbox. The one who chased me down the road.

Then Grandma leaned forward. "Ah-hah!" she shrieked. "There she goes, Mimosa. Cheating our government *again*! See there – going through the door of Genkel and Glimms! No doubt heading for the glamourwear department!"

She leapt up. Waved her hand over one of the small pictures.

It grew bigger. Bigger and bigger and bigger. Until it filled the whole wall. Clear as clear.

I watched Ariadne Von Trinkpott walk in through the huge swing doors of Genkel and Glimms. Then Grandma leapt to the house skychatter. Punched in some numbers. "Edikk," she said. "Genkel and Glimms. Our target is in there. Go now. NOW!"

Grandma sat back down, eyes popping. "I knew it!" she hissed indignantly. "That witch claimed she had shopping to do. Government equipment to buy. But she is *not* shopping for government equipment, Mimosa. She is shopping for robes. For *glamourwear*!"

Grandmas eyes gleamed. "But Edikk will catch her in the act!" she said. "He will leap from the shadows. Snap a picture of Ariadne and her bags of robes. And my Dossier will be almost COMPLETE!"

"What then?" quavered Auntie Mims.

"Then, Mimosa," Grandma said. "I shall surprise her. Reveal Ariadne Von Trinkpott for the lying witch she truly is! Present my Dossier! In Argument House – at Witchministers' Utterings!"

Witchministers' Utterings… Something that happens every Saturday of the year in Argument House. Lots of witchministers sitting on long benches, all making speeches, all arguing with each other about the best way to run United Witchenlands.

Just then Mum swirled out of her office and into the sitting room, talking into her skychatter. "Yes, Miranda," she was saying. "I am aware it is a *risk*, Miranda. But it is also a *chance*. An opportunity. A way to raise our profile. And I MUST take it. No, Miranda – shush. *Shush*. My mind is made up. Goodbye, Miranda."

She swirled over to Grandma.

"Mother," she said briskly. "Our home help will be arriving on Wednesday. You will like her, I promise. She is calm, capable and cheerful. She is perfect."

Grandma just snorted.

"And now," said Mum. "I have a treat for you." Then she flung open the back door and pointed her spellstick.

"*Abrakkida Rune,*" she said.

Lines of magic shot out of her spellstick and down the garden – and there it was. A magicreation. Shimmering – but getting clearer, stronger, all the time.

A soft, pale-green building. Cosy and low. Nestling in its own little corner of the garden, near the gate into the woods…

Grandma's annexe.

Grandma snorted. Again.

"Its a two-hour magicreation, Mother," said Mum. "You can test it out. See if you want changes. And, if you like it, we shall build the real annexe as soon as possible."

Grandma glared at Mum. "I *shall* test my shed, Kristabel," she snapped. "I shall test it thoroughly. But I am warning you – RIGHT NOW – I will *not* like it."

She turned to Auntie Mims. "Mimosa, follow me," she said. Then the two of them stomped off to the back door, noses in the air.

✦

An hour later, I heard crashing noises – very loud ones – coming from the magicreation.

So did Mum. We both raced down the garden, worried something terrible had happened. An accident of some kind.

It hadn't.

We peered in through the window.

Music was blaring in Grandma's kitchen – some olden-days witch warbling an olden-days song – and Auntie Mims was bellowing along.

As for Grandma, she was dashing around the room, brandishing a long stick, thwacking it about. Which was what all the crashing was.

"This is the way, Mimosa!" Grandma was shrieking. "This is how I shall stop Ariadne should she try to escape. I shall HERD her! Herd her towards the witchwardens!"

Then, huffing and puffing, Grandma grabbed two citrijuice cans from the witchchiller. One for her, one for Auntie Mims. She plonked herself down next to Auntie Mims, they clinked their cans, glugged them down – and hurled the empty cans at the bin.

Both cans bounced in.

Grandma and Auntie Mims started cackling, then high-fived...

Just as Mum opened the door.

Straight away, the cackling stopped. Grandma sat bolt upright, and so did Auntie Mims. Both their mouths turned right down.

"So – you like it, then?" said Mum eagerly.

"Kristabel," said Grandma, glaring at her. "It will *do*."

Then she turned to Auntie Mims. "Mimosa," she said. "Follow me. If I am to be *banished* to a shed, I have packing to do."

Then they both stomped off, noses in the air once more. Mum waved her spellstick and – POOF! – the magicreation was gone.

I sniffed. "Mum," I said. "Can you smell that? What is it?"

Because – all of a sudden – I could smell something. A faint smell coming from the woods. A strange smell. A horrible smell. Salty and strong, like the smell of an animal. But mixed with something sweet. Something sickly. Something almost like rotting fruit.

Mum sniffed too. "Drains, I expect," she said. "All that rain we've had lately."

Then I heard faint snapping noises. Faraway noises, also from the woods.

And – even though I *know* nothing big lives in the woods, nothing scary – I walked back up the garden VERY fast.

Chapter 17

Back in the house, Hetty had music blaring out. But not her normal stuff. Not thudding music. Not Shriek Sistaz or Kakkle Kru.

No. Today it was different. Firkelhorns and glinkles. Olden-days music. Not like Hetty. Not at all.

I HAD to know why.

So I knocked – which I always do. It's best with Hetty.

"Inkompel, mien ponkitt sorostinka!" Hetty called out. And even though I haven't studied much Fangwegian, I knew what that meant. Because

Hetty has told me, many times.

So – being her weird little sister – I *did* go in.

Hetty wasn't lolling on her bed, like she usually does. No. Hetty was sitting at her desk, listening intently to the music. "Amadeo Mizzotti, Flo," she said. "A musical genius. Born two hundred and sixty years ago."

Hetty's head was swaying about, and she was trying hard – but not really managing – to tap her foot to Mr Mizzotti's music.

But that wasn't all. Hetty's hair was scraped back. Up in a neat bun on top of her head. And she was wearing specs – which I know she doesn't need. She also had a new outfit. Robes to the knee. Grey robes. Serious-looking.

"Flo," she said, "I have changed my witchsits." Then her specs slipped right down her nose – so she gave up, and took them off.

Hetty is a further learner, just starting further witchsits. Here in South Witchenland, witchteens do five further witchsits. Spell and potion studies, and three more. And first they have Taster Week, where they get to try out different witchsits. See which ones they want to do.

This morning, when Hetty went to college, her Taster Week witchsits were triple frivolities – music, dance and drama.

But not now.

"Flo, I am no longer doing triple frivolities," Hetty said. "I am now doing these." Then she patted three ring binders with big labels on them…

GOVERNMENTALS
WITCHGLOBAL RELATIONS
WITCHDIGGERY

I was amazed. "Governmentals? Witchglobal relations?" I said. "Hetty … are you sure?"

Because Hetty has NEVER been bothered about how Witchworld is run, or what conditions are like for witchworkers, or anything like that – not as long as she can order new robes off the witchweb twenty-four hours a day.

"And … witchdiggery?" I said. "Why witchdiggery?"

Because witchdiggery – digging about for old bones and relics, and finding out what they tell us about witchhistory – was even more baffling. Hetty is always going on about how boring witchhistory is, and she *hates* getting grubby.

"Flo," said Hetty. "I have changed."

I looked at Hetty's eyes. They were shining…

"Hetty," I said. "Have you – by any chance – met a witchboy in college?" I said. "A witchboy doing governmentals, witchglobal relations and witchdiggery?"

"Flo," said Hetty. "I have."

Then the music finished, and Hetty looked relieved. She leaned forward, eyes shining more. "I have found The One, Flo. The *One*," she said. "Errken Padlokk!"

Then she grabbed my arm. "You were right, Flo. I need a witchboy with more depth. Errken has depth. *Lots* of depth!"

Hetty quite often makes me gape when she's talking. She did now.

"And Errken has beautiful green eyes," she said. "And hair that *flops*, Flo, just the way hair should – as *well* as depth, Flo. So *I* must have depth too. I must impress Errken with my depth. Because he is The One, Flo. I know it!"

"Hetty," I said. "I don't know much about this sort of thing – but isn't it better to just be yourself?"

Hetty started cackling so hard I thought she might fall off her chair. "Myself? *Me?*" she said. "No, no, no, Flo. Then Errken won't be interested. Then Errken won't *realise* that I am The One."

Then she leaned forward. Pressed play – and the

137

music started up again.

"Amadeo thingy is Errken's favourite composer," she said. "So I need to listen to Amadeo thingy, Flo. I need to learn to *like* Amadeo thingy."

"But … if Errken is not interested in you as you are," I said, confused, "he's probably not the right witchboy for you."

Hetty threw her head back and did this tinkling cackle she's been practising for weeks. "Flo," she said. "You know so little."

Then she waved her hand. "Now, go. Go! I have a LOT of studying to do." And she brandished a sheet of paper. "I have to study this, Flo. All this. For tomorrow."

At the top the sheet said this…

Things Errken likes

Underneath was a list. A very long list.

"Hetty —" I said. Then I stopped. I could hear a noise in the garden. A loud rasping noise. As if something very big was trying to caw — but had a very sore throat.

And I knew what it was…

A grizzelhump.

Me and Hetty gaped out of the window. Stood utterly still, gaping.

Because I have seen pictures of grizzelhumps, I've seen them on the witchscreen – on *Wild and Wonderful Witchglobe* – but *never* in real life.

They're rare. Extremely rare birds, even in Witchenwild, where they live.

The grizzelhump was huge. A lot bigger than me. A lot bigger than a grown-up. Bald head – shiny bright blue – and a big red beak. A long skinny neck, and a long skinny body – all covered in big black feathers. Two bulky black humps on its back, and huge orange wings.

It was standing at the bottom of the garden, near the gate to the woods, wings folded by its sides, head jerking as it looked around nervously.

Grizzelhumps are timid. Scared of witches – which is a very good thing. Because a grizzelhump could pick up a witchkid in its huge claws and fly off with it. Easily.

"Frea-ky," whispered Hetty. "What's it *doing* here?"

Then she got out her skychatter. "I am SO getting a picture and sending it to Gigi," she said. And she clicked.

The grizzelhump's head swivelled round. It stared

up the garden with its shiny black eyes and – with one flap of its huge orange wings – it was gone.

But Hetty was right. It was freaky. To see a grizzelhump, here in South Witchenland – it was astonishing…

And a little bit strange.

Chapter 18

First lesson on Tuesday was Fangwegian.

Wherever you live – Sniddgroll in the Shiverlands, Oggentakk in the Narrowlands, a colony in the Grimlands where witchkids actually go to school – you probably learn Fangwegian.

I think it's because Fangway is such a big and important colony that we all learn Fangwegian. I think witches in Fangway expect it. Think we should all speak their language, so they don't have to bother learning ours.

Which is, in my opinion, a bit rude and lazy of them – however rich and powerful Fangway is.

Still, it's what happens.

Emerald Class did a Fangwegian Taster Term at the end of last year. But now, this year – we're beginning Fangwegian properly.

Hetty warned me about it. "Yawnsome, totally, at your level," she said. "Gazillions of words to copy off the greenboard. Gazillions of tests. Deadly dull."

Well – it was NOT deadly dull. Not the way Mr Prankett taught it.

He marched in. Beamed round the whole room. "Hikkel vartt, Emerald Class," he said. "Ompel prink."

"Hikkel vartt, Mr Prankett," we all chorused. Then we all sat down.

Because we got as far as good morning and sit down last term – but not a lot further.

"Bumm," said Mr Prankett, nodding and looking pleased. Then he tapped the greenboard. And some words appeared...

Nonkel	Nose
Argel	Eye
Orgel	Ear
Krimp	Mouth
Ginkon	Arm

Dink	Hand
Stronkon	Leg
Lonk	Foot

"*Abrakkida Rune*," Mr Prankett said, pointing his spellstick.

We all gasped. Because there, in the middle of our classroom, a shimmering shape was appearing. Growing bigger and bigger. A huge lumbering creature, with goggling eyes, and whiskers, and a spiny tail that wrapped itself halfway round the classroom.

We gaped. We giggled. We shivered. We all knew what it was.

A thrumbulger – from "The Thrumbulger Thrashing of Thripp", one of the *Magical Myths*.

Mamie's hand shot up. "Mr Prankett, I hope that is a magimirage, and NOT a magicreation," she said sternly. "Because if that is a magicreation – even if it is only a two-minute magicreation – it could actually hurt us."

"Fear not, Mamie," said Mr Prankett. "This is indeed a magimirage. It is only an image. Although it looks real, it is NOT real. Not a magicreation." And he stuck his arm through the thrumbulger, just to prove it.

Then Mr Prankett pointed his spellstick. A beam of light shot out of the end and lit up the thrumbulger's nose.

"Nonkel," Mr Prankett shouted — as the thrumbulger sneezed.

He pointed his spellstick again. Another beam of light shot out. This one lit up the thrumbulger's eye.

"Argel!" Mr Prankett shouted — and the thrumbulger blinked.

Next, a beam of light shot on to the thrumbulger's huge ear — and Mr Prankett looked at us with his eyebrows raised.

"Orgel," we all shouted, as the thrumbulger flapped its ear, like it was trying to get rid of an annoying wizzel.

By the end of the lesson we knew sixteen body parts in Fangwegian — including toenails, warts and whiskers.

Mr Prankett based every lesson that day round *Magical Myths*.

In words, he read us "The Dredgeboggle Stampede of South Strigg". And we debated the best course of action for a witchkid faced with stampeding dredgeboggles in the mall.

In numbers, we had questions like this:

Emerald Class go on an outing to the Singing Stillwaters.

There are 18 witchchildren, 1 witchteacher, 3 full picnic hampers and 1 half-full picnic hamper.

Unfortunately, the seven-tusked Oglestomp is also on an outing to the Singing Stillwaters. And the Oglestomp is hungry... Very hungry.

It takes the Oglestomp 2.5 hours to crunch 1 witchchild, 3.5 hours to crunch a witchteacher, and I hour to crunch a full picnic hamper.

How long will it take the Oglestomp to crunch Emerald Class, their witchteacher and their picnic hampers?

Then, last lesson before dinner was witchhistory.

"Emerald Class," said Mr Prankett, "our Class Directive is one local study and one global study. We shall start with the local study. The Hovelhaggs."

The Hovelhaggs have ruled United Witchenlands

for hundreds of years.

Once me and Mum saw the Hovelhaggs – the current Esteemed Graciouswitch and all the mini-Graciouswitches – scudding past us on Skyway 1 in their royal skysquanderer, heading for Hovelhagg Palace.

Because the Hovelhaggs have four palaces. One each in Witchenfinn, Witchenwail and Witchenwild. And, just outside Haggspit, the biggest palace of all. Hovelhagg Palace.

"So…" said Mr Prankett. "The Hovelhaggs. Are they any use, or should we get rid of them?"

There was a gasp from every single witchkid in class.

"Mr Prankett," said Mamie, frowning. "That is disrespectful. The Hovelhaggs are our rulers."

"Yes, Mamie," said Mr Prankett, "they are our rulers – but what do they do that's useful?"

We all sat and thought. They're very rich, our Hovelhaggs – but they don't do much. They don't run the colony. Not like the First Witchminister, and her Deputy Witchminister and all the other witchministers.

Then Mervikk's hand shot up. "They marry their cousins in colonies like Drakken and Lakktarn," he said, jiggling hard. "And when they get married, we have a day off school. So that's VERY useful."

"And," said Henka Sprigg, "there was a new Esteemed Graciouswitchbaby two months ago. And that meant lots of work for witchnannies. So that's useful."

Then Mamie Swip's hand shot up. "They bring tourists to United Witchenlands, Mr Prankett," she said. "That's useful."

"And you can visit their palaces and buy things," said Juno Rinkbott. "Useful things, like mugs and tea towels with their faces on."

"You can indeed visit their palaces, Juno," said Mr Prankett.

Then he pointed his spellstick – and a shimmering magimirage appeared. Of a painting. A huge painting that stretched out sideways right across the classroom.

"Inside Hovelhagg Palace," Mr Prankett said, "is this painting. One of the most famous paintings in the whole of Witchworld. It is called 'The Haggfiend Chooses her Victim'."

I shivered.

It was a terrifying painting – but beautiful too. A mix of dark shadows and strong light. Showing all the little Graciouswitches, playing in the Coronation Courtyard. And – in the background, peeking out from behind a pillar – the huge figure of the Haggfiend. All in shadows. Just light on her face. On her glinting yellow eyes. On her huge hooked nose. On her thin cruel mouth, curved up in a grin as she stared at the little Graciouswitches. Picking. Choosing. Deciding which one to snatch.

"This was painted hundreds of years ago," said Mr Prankett. "By a painter called Remm Van Brantokk. His imagination was fired by *Magical Myths*, just as ours are. And now you, Emerald Class, are going to do a copy of it."

Mamie's hand shot up. "Mr Prankett," she tutted. "Copying a painting is NOT witchhistory. It is frivolities. Art frivolities. And we are only supposed to do frivolities once a week."

Which is true. Last year we did frivolities – music, art, dance or drama – every day. But this year the government has decided frivolities is not proper learning.

"Mamie," said Mr Prankett, brandishing the *Manual of Best Practice* in one hand. "It says here *Competition is to be keenly encouraged among students.* And this, Mamie, IS a competition."

Then he held up a whoopee cushion, with the Hovelhagg coat of arms on it. "Best drawing wins this," he said.

Which was how Mervikk ended up winning a whoopee cushion.

Last thing before lunchtime – just after Mr Prankett had to confiscate Mervikk's whoopee cushion until going-home time – Mr Prankett got us all acting out a scene from "Haggfiend Horror".

It was the scene where Queen Hinkel the First realises the smallest Graciouswitch has been snatched. The scene where she sends out the proclamation, offering the reward for getting rid of the Haggfiend.

And that scene is special to me. Because Dad used to do a brilliant imitation of Queen Hinkel the First realising her precious little Graciouswitch is gone. And thinking about Dad pretending to be a distressed Esteemed Graciouswitch, wringing his hands, and sobbing, and screaming…

Thinking about that – it gave me the Aches.

149

Chapter 19

The Aches are nasty, like grabbing things. The Aches creep up on me. Attack with no warning. Grab me out of nowhere.

The Aches make me want to crawl away and hide…

So I did.

As soon as the screecher went for lunchtime, I headed straight to the roberooms. I shut myself in a cubicle, put my head in my hands and waited for the Aches to go away.

So I sat there, I don't know exactly how long – I never do with the Aches – then I heard the roberoom door open.

Then I heard a voice, Lily's, sounding worried. "Are you sure you'll be all right, Ferocity?"

"Yes," said a sad, sniffing voice. "I'll be fine. It's just... Being new. Being in school. Off the streets. It's all, well – a bit much to take in. I just need a little time alone."

"I understand," said Kika's voice now, and I could hear her patting Ferocity's hand. "There are times in life when—"

"We BOTH understand," said Lily. "We do. Totally. We'll be outside. Take as long as you want."

"Thanks," said that sad, sniffing voice. "I am SO glad I have you two to help me."

Then Lily and Kika left. And I heard footsteps, then a bag unzipping and some rustling. And then Ferocity's voice, muttering and sniffing. "Stupid *stupid* witchgirls..."

Which was when I opened my cubicle door.

*

Ferocity whipped round – and gasped. Clasped her hand to her mouth.

And I had to ask her. I just couldn't help it. "Why did you say that? Stupid stupid witchgirls?"

Ferocity looked at me. Bit her lip. "So ... you heard that, then?" she said, staring down at the floor.

"Yes," I said. "Why did you say it?"

Ferocity bit her lip more. Then she looked up, looked straight at me, eyelashes fluttering over big sad eyes. "I … I don't know exactly," she said. "I know it was wrong."

Then her mouth started wobbling. "It's just – it's hard. Being with you. All such lucky witchgirls," she said. "Maybe I'm a bit, well … *jealous*. All these years I've been struggling. On the streets. And all of you – happy. Safe."

Her mouth wobbled more. "And I'm just not *used* to having friends," she said, with a sniff. "Not many friends on the street."

She was an astonishing actress. Good as a witchscreen star.

But it was all lies, I *knew* it was. Because I don't tell lies myself – I just can't – but I'm good at spotting when other witchgirls do.

And I had to say something, so I did. "Thing is," I said, "all the orphan stuff. The teaching yourself in libraries. The fried gutter nibbets. All that – I don't really believe it's true."

Maybe that was the wrong thing to say, but I said it. And now I'd said it, I couldn't quite stop. I had to say more.

"It's like you're acting. Lying," I said. "Pretending

to be an orphan. But I don't know why."

I saw Ferocity's mouth drop open. Saw her face change. "Acting? Lying?" she said. "Why would I be doing that? *Why?*"

And her voice had gone all shrill. Nervous. She seemed to be almost ... well – panicking.

"I don't know," I said. "But you *shouldn't* lie. Not about being a homeless orphan. Because being a homeless orphan is a REAL thing, an actual thing, a *sad* thing. And I don't think actual homeless orphans would be *at all* happy with a witchgirl pretending to be one."

Ferocity glared at me. "I am NOT acting, NOT lying," she hissed. "I am an *orphan*. From the streets. Who has had the VERY GOOD LUCK to be plucked out of the gutter."

Then she turned to go, grabbed her bag off the shelf – and something fell out and on to the floor.

She tried to snatch it up.

Too late. I had already grabbed it.

I stared down. It was a picture. A mum. A dad. A small chunky witchtoddler. And a witchboy, about six. All smiling. Laughing.

"That ... is that your *family*?" I said, gaping. "That witchboy – he looks like you. Is he your brother?"

She snatched it back. "No, he is NOT," she said.

Then she looked at me, eyes glinting hard. Grey as Witchenwater on a stormy winter day.

"And," she hissed, leaning towards me and snapping, right in my face, "if you dare to say that I am acting, that I am lying, that I am *not* an orphan – to any other witchgirl in Emerald Class – you will be EXTREMELY sorry."

Now, that shocked me. And also made me annoyed. "Are you threatening me?" I said.

"Yes," said Ferocity, then she stuck her nose in the air and marched out of the roberoom.

Chapter
20

After school I had a firkelhorn lesson, so I took Skybus 62 and flew to Haggspit Music Centre.

By the time I got home, the sky was growing dark. Raindrops were pattering down. Then thunder started grumbling in the distance.

I went to my bedroom and lifted the lid off my buzzfish tank. Out they all shot – first Godril, then Bink and Anemone and, last of all, Kassandra.

I do like my buzzfish, but they're not cuddly. Not soft, fluffy pets. Not pets I can sit on my lap, and stroke, and tell things to – which is the sort of pet I'd really like.

So I sat there, watching my buzzfish zooming around the room. Listening to the rain, drumming down harder and harder. The thunder, growing louder and louder.

After a while, I got my buzzfish whistle and blew it. "Back in the tank," I said.

Sometimes my buzzfish ignore the whistle, and I have to chase them around the room, trying to catch them. But not today. Today they buzzed straight over to the tank, and dived back in. So I put the lid back on.

The storm was right above the house now. Rain was hurling itself at the windows. Then a big flash of lightning lit up the whole room. And thunder boomed out.

That was when I heard it. A small scratching noise. Scratch scratch scratch. Right outside my window.

And there it was again. Scratch scratch scratch.

I looked out.

Saw a small head – drenched and bedraggled – a drooping mouth and sad blue eyes, staring in at me.

The troll baby.

Quivering. Crawking. Scratching at the window with his paws. Desperate to get in.

✳

The troll was soaking. He was shivering. And he

was VERY smelly…

He was also small enough to fit in the bathroom basin.

I used Hetty's pomegranate shower gel. Lathered him up, until big soapy bubbles frothed and foamed all over his fur. Then I rinsed him off with lots of warm water. I rinsed and I rinsed and I rinsed.

The troll did NOT like being lathered, or rinsed.

He glared. He hissed. He wriggled. He struggled. He spat. He tried to bite my fingers off. And he crawked and he crawked and he crawked.

But I carried on. Until at last, the water was filthy but the troll was clean. Then I lifted him out, wrapped him up and towel-dried him.

"There," I said, putting him on the bathroom floor. "All clean, all dry."

The troll stood, glaring up at me. Very small, very cross, very fluffy – and gnashing his teeth…

Which was when Mum walked past.

She let out a shriek. Ran in. "Shoo!" she shrieked, waving her hands. "Shoo! Get out, get out!"

The troll just stood there, folded his paws. Tapped his foot and hissed at her.

"Mum," I said. "Can I keep him? Look after him? Make him my pet?"

"Certainly not," Mum shrieked. "That creature is

a PEST! Vermin!"

There was a snort from the door. "He is a baby, Kristabel," said Grandma. "And your ejecting spell has left this troll with no family. We have a *duty* to look after him."

She turned to me. "Flo," she said. "Troll taming. Some tips. First, hand signals. Very important."

She looked down at the troll. "Sit," she said firmly, holding her hand up. "SIT."

The troll stared up at her.

Then Hetty stuck her head round the door. Gaped. "Gigi HAS to see this!" she shrieked. She crouched down on the floor, next to the troll. Got out her skychatter and took a picture.

Then she shrieked more, and leapt up. Fast.

There was a puddle. A small puddle spreading across the floor. A small puddle that smelt of ... well – *troll*.

★

So I carried the troll to my bedroom. Got Astribel out of my cupboard.

Astribel – my favourite dolly of all. With curly black hair, bright-green eyes, and a small snub nose.

Astribel was a present on my third birthday. She has curly black hair, bright green eyes, and she came in a box with a cot, a bottle of pretend kronkel-milk, three sets of robes, two onesies – and a potty.

First, I showed Astribel to the troll.

"Troll –" I said. Then I stopped. I couldn't call him *Troll*. That wasn't a name. But … what to call him? Not an Otto. Definitely not an Otto. But what? Bodrik? Anvil? Tronk? Nothing seemed quite right.

The troll stood there, glaring at me.

"This is Astribel," I said. "She is a very special dolly. She's a witchbaby – just like you are a troll baby."

The troll hissed. Then he crawked.

"Astribel can do this," I said, and I pressed her belly button.

Astribel cried. Then she gurgled. Then she spoke. "I love you, Mummy," she said.

The troll growled. He backed away. Bared his tiny sharp teeth. His fur slowly turned the colour of my walls. And I knew why. He sensed danger. He was trying to hide. To camouflage himself.

He failed.

A small troll backing away, fur bristling – even a small troll now the colour of my walls – was still clear as clear.

Then I showed the troll Astribel's potty. "Astribel has a potty," I said. "And when Astribel wants to make a puddle, she uses it."

I sat Astribel on the potty. I pressed the middle of her back – and Astribel demonstrated how to fill the potty.

I showed my troll the contents of the potty. "See," I said, pointing. "Puddles go in here. Not on the floor."

The troll grabbed the potty. Turned it upside down, emptied it then hurled it across the room.

I thought it might be hunger making him so grumpy – because hunger always makes *me* grumpy. So I got him a drink and some food. Things I thought a troll might like.

A carton of glimberry shivershake. A banana. And a lump of kronkel-milk cheese.

He grabbed the carton and gnawed a chunk out of it. He watched the shivershake spill out on to the floor, then ate the carton.

He also ate the banana. The whole thing, including the skin.

He took one bite of the kronkel-milk cheese, and spat it out. Then he hurled the rest of the lump at me.

So I gave up. Made him a cosy nest in Astribel's cot. Lifted him up, tucked Astribel's soft blanket around him, then put the cot by my bed.

And the troll must have been tired, because he gave one last glare. One last cross crawk. Then his eyes closed, his mouth opened, and he started to snore.

Chapter 21

I went into the kitchen, and found Grandma watching *Haggnews*. Hetty was, too – which surprised me. Because Hetty NEVER watches *Haggnews*.

But she was watching today. Peering out from behind her specs, leaning forward, listening hard, taking notes.

Haggnews was reporting from a witchdiggery site in Lower Haggspit. Witchdiggers had found bones, lots of them, and put them all together, laid them all out.

There were bits of bone missing, but whatever the bones belonged to – it was HUGE. With a very long tail, a very wide rib cage and an enormous skull.

Hetty took a picture of the bones on her skychatter. Then she leapt up. "I must share this with Errken," she said. "Errken must know what a keen interest I am taking in witchdiggery developments in our local area."

Then she rushed out of the kitchen and off to her bedroom.

I sat down next to Grandma. The chief witchdigger was being interviewed on *Haggnews*. Saying they hadn't yet identified the creature. That it might be some type of dragon. Or even a brand-new species.

Grandma sat there, snorting. "That is NOT a brand-new species. It's a very *old* species," she said.

Now the chief witchdigger was showing a mock-up of what the creature might have looked like, and the slow lumbering way it might have walked. Saying it was an intriguing puzzle waiting to be solved.

Grandma snorted again. "Nitwit. LOOK at it, you silly witchman," she said. "Look at the size … the shape … the bones … the skull … the way it walks… Everything. That is *not* an intriguing puzzle waiting to be solved. It is not a puzzle at all. It is clearly – CLEARLY – a thrumbulger!"

Then Grandma turned to me. "Great big lumbering things, Mummy said they were," she said. "She saw over fifty of them – all lumbering about in her Shudders. Some of the clearest Shudders Mummy *ever* had!"

The Shudders…

The Shudders were something Great-Grandma – Grandma's mother – could do. She could stand on a spot where important witchhistory had happened, and Shudder. And as she Shuddered, she would see the witchhistory that happened there, unfolding right in front of her eyes.

She saw witchhistory like the Charge of the Cave Witches, and the Battle of Banshee Bridge. Things witches *know* actually happened.

But that wasn't all Great-Grandma saw with her Shudders. No. Because she also saw The Deadly Dodger Attack on Drool, The Honkbottle Invasion of Itchasnitch, and The Globegobbler Guzzle of Gormwitt – and The Thrumbulger Thrashing of Thripp...

All from *Magical Myths of the Witchenlands*.

That – according to Grandma – proves all the myths are real. Actual witchhistory. That they actually happened, just as the Charge of the Cave Witches did.

But I'm not so sure Grandma is right.

"Grandma," I said. "It is *possible* that the Shudders are some form of Confusions. That Great-Grandma saw bits of witchhistory and bits of myths."

Grandma turned, eyes popping. "There was NOTHING confused about Mummy's Shudders, Flo," she said. "She saw witchhistory – and that is that."

Then her eyes narrowed. She peered hard at me. "Flo," she said. "Are you still worrying about the Shudders? Worrying you might have some form of Confusions?"

"A bit," I said…

Because I Shudder too. I am the second Skritchett Shudderer.

Well, I Shuddered once.

But when I Shuddered, I didn't see past witchhistory. I saw *future* witchhistory. I saw the ghoul attack.

And the Shudders were horrible things. Terrifying feelings that started in my middle and squirmed through every bit of me. So I'm hoping I NEVER Shudder again – and I *haven't*. Not yet.

But, still, I can't help thinking about the Shudders,

even though I don't *want* to think about them. I worry they might be some form of Confusions.

And the more I think about the Shudders, the more questions I have. Because there's a LOT that I don't understand. Especially this...

"Grandma," I said. "Witchhistory, big events – past or future – they must happen everywhere. In lots of places. So why didn't Great-Grandma Shudder all the time? And why don't I? Why don't I *keep* Shuddering? Why just once? Just then?"

"Because," said Grandma, eyes gleaming, "the Shudders are *capricious*, Flo!"

"Capricious?" I said.

"They are unpredictable. They work in their own way," Grandma said. "They behave how they want to behave. Sometimes they show things. Sometimes not."

Grandma shook her head. "Even Mummy never really understood her Shudders," she said. "Once Mummy stood on the very ground where the Seventh Siege of Shivergrim took place – for *three whole days*, Flo. She saw NOTHING! Not one thing!"

Grandma looked at me, eyes gleaming. "The Shudders are strange and mysterious things," she said. "But the one thing the Shudders are – is *truthful*."

"But why are you so sure, Grandma?" I said. "That the Shudders are truthful? That they only show real things? That they prove the myths are real witchhistory?"

"Because of the way in which Mummy first got her Shudders," Grandma said, eyes gleaming.

Then she leaned closer. "Besides," she said, "those Shudders of Mummy's, they are not the *only* proof the myths are real witchhistory. There is the Blob too."

"The Blob?" I said.

"The Blob on the original manuscript of the *Magical Myths*," said Grandma. "The Blob that—"

But just then we heard shrieking.

"My snug!" Mum was shrieking. "What has that creature done to my SNUG?"

Chapter 22

I sprinted to Mum's snug, Grandma close behind.

We stood in the doorway and gaped. There were sticks. Sticks EVERYWHERE. On the sofa, on the floor, everywhere. Huge piles of sticks from the garden. Big sticks, small sticks, all kinds of sticks.

The snug window was wide open. And – oh dear – my troll was *not* safely tucked up in Astribel's cot, snoring. Not any more. He was padding up the garden, clasping another stick in his paws. A chunky, heavy-looking one.

As for Mum, she was standing in the middle

of the snug, wringing her hands and wailing. "What has he done?" she wailed. "What has he DONE?"

"He is preparing to *build*, Kristabel," said Grandma. "All trolls build dens. It is perfectly normal."

"But *not* in my snug," Mum wailed. "No building – not in my SNUG!"

"Kristabel, you really are a fusspot," said Grandma, tutting. "You hardly ever use the snug. You're far too busy."

"One more stick inside this house," hissed Mum, "and that troll GOES!"

"Have no fear, Kristabel," said Grandma grandly. "I shall train him."

She turned to me. "Flo," she said. "Watch. And learn."

And she turned to the window as the small fluffy head of my troll appeared. He heaved himself up on to the windowsill, stick still clasped in his paws. Then he saw all of us, standing in the snug, staring at him.

He stared back.

"No," said Grandma firmly, shaking her head and holding up her hand, palm out. "NO sticks in the snug."

My troll stared more. Then he hopped down into

the room, still carrying the stick.

"Very well," Grandma said, pursing her lips. "So be it."

She pointed her wand. "*Abrakkida Mutattikk, Bakkuliki Mutik, Diversikka, Optikka, Lune,*" she said, in the strange singsong voice she uses to do spells. "*Ambik Non, Elsik Non, Revikkto Zin Rovvik, Ignittik, Bestolikka, Grune.*"

A shower of stardust burst out of her wand and headed straight for the stick.

My troll yelped. He dropped the stick as if it was burning hot. And – with a *zizz* – the stick was gone. Transformed into a buzzing red insect with long flaming pincers.

"A firehopper," cackled Grandma, watching it fly out of the window, trailing smoke behind it. "That troll will soon learn not to bring sticks into the house."

My troll did NOT like his stick being turned into a firehopper. He threw a tantrum. He hurled himself on the floor. He bawled. He drummed his feet on the ground. He gnashed his teeth. He changed colour. From orange to purple, red to blue, green to yellow. He was furious with rage.

"Leave him be, Flo," said Grandma, turning her back on him. "He is simply seeking attention. And now, follow me – I have something for you."

I stared down at the narrow case, shining and silver. I knew straight away what was in there…

One of Grandma's wands.

I opened the case, and there it was. Jiggling quietly. Grandma's short stubby wand.

I picked the wand up – and it glowed.

"It remembers you," said Grandma, eyes gleaming. "Remembers what you did."

Well, I remembered too.

Because me and that wand – that small stubby wand – we helped stop the ghoul attack. We saved Hetty and all her friends. Saved all the witchteens from being turned into ghouls.

"That wand and I, we *never* got on," said Grandma. "It will have a far better home with you."

Her eyes gleamed. She leaned forward. "I do believe this is a one-witch wand, Flo," she said.

"A one-witch wand?" I said.

"A wand that attaches itself to only one witch. A wand that will work for one witch alone. And *you*, Flo, are that witch. The wand has chosen you. In another witch's hands, this wand will backsurge – just as it did with me."

I remembered how the wand backsurged. How

it refused to do Grandma's spell. How it turned itself into a huge squawking bird – and knocked Grandma out.

But…

"Grandma," I said. "I'm not supposed to have a wand."

Because, I don't know what laws your colony has about wands – but here in South Witchenland we have *very* strict laws. And us witchkids are NOT allowed wands.

Grandma snorted. "Only good can come from you having this wand," she said. "You are entirely to be trusted. You would do no witch-harming magic, no mayhem magic, no mocking magic – no criminal magic of ANY KIND with it. You and this wand, you are a *team*."

And, as I sat there, the wand glowed in my hand. Felt warm, felt happy. Started making tiny purring sounds.

I thought about Dad. How he thought the law was wrong. "All witchchildren should learn to use a wand," he said. "It is their heritage, their witchhistory."

I remembered how Dad still kept a wand himself. How Dad would sit listening to Grandma for hours. Telling him tales of where and when she got each of her wands. Showing him spells.

And what he told Hetty one time, when she was laughing at Grandma. "Just because witches have new magic ways," he told her, "does not mean we should forget all the old magic ways."

So...

"Thank you, Grandma," I said. "I'll look after it. Treasure it."

"Oh, you'll do more than that," said Grandma briskly. "You'll *use* it. Right now. It won't take you long to learn the spell – after all, you know the basics."

The witches in charge of this book have asked me once again to point out that they IN NO WAY encourage witchchildren to break any of the magic laws of Witchworld.

Grandma was right. It didn't take long. Because I *did* know the basics. I'd done a transforming spell before. I transformed Hetty and the witcheens into nibbets, to save them from the ghouls. And this transforming spell – to transform a stick into a firehopper – used some of the same words.

Grandma gave me lots of help too. Gave me tips on all the wandwaving, and on the special singsong voice to use for the words.

So when my troll came padding up the garden with another huge stick – I was ready for him.

I pointed the wand. "*Abrakkida Mutattikk, Bakkuliki Mutik, Diversikka, Optikka, Lune,*" I said, fast as I could. "*Ambik Non, Elsik Non, Revikkto Zin Rovvik, Ignittik, Bestolikka, Grune.*"

A shower of stardust burst out of my wand and headed straight for the stick. And, once again, my troll yelped, and dropped the stick. Then it turned into a firehopper, and was gone.

"Bravo!" said Grandma, clapping and beaming. "You are your father's daughter, Flo. A gifted learner, just as he was."

Three times my troll tried to bring a stick into the snug. Three times I did the spell. Three times he hurled himself to the floor and bawled.

But not the fourth time.

The fourth time, he padded up the garden with another knobbly stick clasped in his paws. He heaved himself up on to the windowsill. Saw me pointing the wand. And he stopped.

He stared. He glared. He gave the stick a grumpy sort of push with his foot – and it dropped back down into the garden behind him. Then he hopped down into the snug, stomped out of the door, and off to my bedroom.

✦

I went into my bedroom a bit later – and gaped.

My troll had been exploring. Every corner of my room. Every drawer. Every cupboard. Every shelf.

He'd been scribbling on the walls with my gel pens. And all over the walls, all over the ceiling, there were small sticky sucker marks.

I knew why.

Because urban trolls have paws that can stick. Paws with small sticky suction pads underneath. So urban trolls can run up anything. A wheelie bin. A drainpipe. A brick wall. Anything.

Including a bedroom ceiling.

Now my troll was under my desk, sulking. He'd made a den for himself. Draped a blanket over the desk, and dragged Astribel's cot inside. Hidden things from all over my room in there. Books, socks, pens. Most of them chewed, including my magiography homework book.

So I checked the witchweb. Looked for advice on troll taming. And there *was* advice. It was this…

Do NOT, under any circumstances, try to tame an urban troll. They are WILD CREATURES. They canNOT be tamed.

Just then, my witchfixer beeped.

I had a Kwikpik coming in – a Kwikpik of Lily. Floating around her bedroom on her bedside rug, eating a chocolate Krunch'n'Munch.

With text underneath: *Snacky-time!*

I felt my heart sink. Because Lily was not the only witchgirl on the rug, floating and eating a chocolate Krunch'n'Munch. Ferocity was there too...

Wearing a Clubbies badge.

Chapter 23

I was *not* happy with Lily next morning. And the moment she came up the skybus stairs, I told her so.

"Clubbies," I said, as she squashed on the seat with me and Kika. "You should have asked. Checked before you got Ferocity to join."

There was a gasp from Kika. "Lily, did you do that? Did you?"

Because Kika has a ban – no witchfixer or skychatter in the evenings. Ever since Kika's mum found Kika still on GoGlobe at two in the morning. Busy looking at clips of witchcelebs falling over and making fools of themselves.

Lily got a shifty, guilty sort of look on her face. "I don't see why you're fussing," she said. "Ferocity is new. She needs friends."

"*Still*," I said, "you should have asked. Clubbies is all of us. That's the whole point of it. You can't do Clubbies without us."

Then me and Lily sat, frowning at each other, as Kika sat between us, eyebrows knotted.

And Kika has the sort of face that shows exactly what she's thinking. Which was this…

First, it was bad that Lily did Clubbies without us. But second, it was also *good* she did Clubbies without us, because now Ferocity was in Clubbies. And third, me and Lily should stop glaring at each other – because Kika likes everyone to be friends.

So Kika turned to Lily. "Lils," she said sternly. "Flo is right. You should have asked. Checked."

Then she turned to me. "Flo," she said, also sternly. "Lils is also right. It was an act of kindness. After all, Ferocity is an orphan. She has had a life of challenges."

Then she sat back, nodding. "So you're both right," she said, looking like everything was sorted. But I had a feeling it wasn't.

I was right.

★

Ferocity rushed over, beaming, as we walked in through the playground gates – the Clubbies badge pinned to her robes.

"I am so HAPPY," she said, eyes shining. "I never *imagined* things this good could happen to me. Being in Clubbies, it makes me feel really, well – part of the gang!"

Then she reached in her robe pocket. "So I made these last night," she said, bringing out bracelets. Four of them. All matching.

"One each," she said, handing them round.

"Clubbie bracelets," gasped Kika. "Matching bracelets! To go with our matching badges!"

She put hers on straight away, and admired it on her wrist. So did Lily.

I stared down at the bracelet in my hand, not sure what to think. Worried Ferocity might be up to something – but what?

Then I found out.

She turned towards me, and spoke. "Flo," she said, in a small, anxious voice, "don't you like your bracelet? Don't you want it?"

She bit her lip. "Or is it … do you not want me in Clubbies?" she said. "It was *your* idea, after all. So … do you *mind* that Lily asked me to join? Did you want Clubbies to be just the three of you?"

I knew I should speak. Put the bracelet on. Pretend I loved it. Pretend I was happy Ferocity was in Clubbies. But I couldn't. I just could NOT pretend.

Because I could see what Lily and Kika couldn't.

Ferocity's eyes glinting as she looked at me.

Then Lily butted in. "Of *course* Flo doesn't mind," she said. "And you know what? I think we should have a Clubbie sleepover. This weekend."

Now Kika was nodding hard. "The four of us," she said, beaming. "With our Clubbie badges and bracelets."

Ferocity plastered a thrilled sort of look across her face. Then, wiping it off, she turned towards me. "Is that OK with you, Flo?" she said anxiously. "Say if it isn't."

I knew what she was up to. Planting the idea in Lily and Kika's heads that I did NOT want Ferocity in Clubbies. That I did NOT want her to be our friend.

Which I didn't – but only because I knew she was lying.

Then it got worse. Because a voice started shouting. "Ferocity, Ferocity! How are you settling in?"

We turned. Witchpaps were outside the

playground gates. Snapping pictures of Ferocity.

Three witchteachers rushed to shoo the witchpaps away – but Ferocity spotted another opportunity.

And she seized it.

She turned to me. "Flo," she said, sounding worried, "I hope it doesn't bother you, the witchpaps being here for me, not you."

Then she gave me a big beaming smile. "Silly me, of course you don't mind," she said, shaking her head. "You're not the sort of witchgirl to be jealous."

She linked her arm through mine. "And maybe you can give me some tips," she said, still beaming. "On how you handled the witchpaps. Back when *you* were the celebrity, not me."

I couldn't help it. I shrugged her off. She was sneaky. Trying to make me look jealous of all the attention on her. And, worst of all, it was working.

Because Lily, Kika – they were looking at me as I shrugged her off. Both with small puzzled frowns.

Then, last lesson before lunchtime, Ferocity did it again.

✦

"*Abrakkida Rune*," said Mr Prankett, standing at the front of the class, and pointing his spellstick straight at himself.

There was a flash of light, and we all gasped. Gone were Mr Prankett's normal witchteacher robes. Now he was wearing stiff black robes that stuck out sideways, with patterns – red, green and yellow – on the top half. He had a hard round red hat on his head, attached under his chin.

"Greets, Emerald Class," he boomed, in a very loud voice, speaking Witchen – sort of – with a very strange accent. "I am name Igbord Stronk. Visiting witchteacher. From Gluggen in Gruntledagg."

We all gaped. Gluggen, capital of Gruntledagg – a colony in the Shiverlands, as you probably know.

Then Mr Prankett bowed. "Class will kindly be excuse my Witchen biffboffs," he said. "Gruntledagg speak is Shiverikkan."

He gave a twirl. "Class must admire outfit. Is colony costume. Witchteachers in Gruntledagg is all wear colony costume to teach."

Mamie stuck her hand up. "Mr Prankett, you are NOT actually a visiting witchteacher from Gruntledagg," she said severely. "You are pretending. And I don't think that's allowed."

Mr Prankett stared at Mamie. "Small witchgirl with cross face," he said. "Subject of lesson is witchcitizenship. Study of witchy ways in Gruntledagg. And Class Directive – signed by *most* eminent witch – say witchteacher must make all effort to increase witchchild understanding of colony culture."

Then he looked round the class. "Learning will be Gruntledagg way," he said. "And witchchildren in Gruntledagg is always end morning by singing."

Mamie's hand shot up again. "That's all very well, Mr Prankett," she said sternly. "But singing is *not* witchcitizenship. Singing is frivolities."

Then Mervikk's hand shot up. "Mr Prankett," he said, jiggling and fidgeting.

Mr Prankett stared straight at Mervikk. "Is small fidget witchboy meaning Mr Stronk?" he said.

"Mr Stronk," said Mervikk, jiggling more. "Flo's got a really lovely voice. Best in class."

Mr Prankett swivelled to stare at me. And it's true. I can sing. When I sing, I forget to be shy. Forget to be nervous. Forget everything.

"Gruntledagg colony anthem is tiptop tune," Mr Prankett said, nodding proudly. "Small witchgirl must sing bellows."

Then he pointed his spellstick once more. "*Abrakkida Rune*," he said.

Straight away, the black and green keys of the pianodrone started to bob up and down, bashing out a tune. And some very strange words – Shiverikkan words – scribbled themselves all over the greenboard.

Mr Prankett started to march round the classroom, singing loudly. And we all marched behind him, joining in.

The tune was easy to pick up, so my voice soared out…

And so did another voice, right in front of me.

Ferocity's. Pure and strong and clear.

Now – maybe this should have been the point where me and Ferocity began to be friends. Had a shared interest. Something we could both do.

It wasn't.

Because, as we got to the end of the anthem, my voice and Ferocity's both soaring out - she gave a sudden lurch sideways. Stopped singing, and let out a loud shocked screech. Then she fell to the floor, knocking her arm on a table as she fell.

She picked herself up, gasping and holding her arm. Got to her feet, then looked at me and spoke. "It's OK, Flo," she said bravely. "I'm sure you didn't *mean* to push me."

And Lily, Kika – they both stared at me. As the frowns on their faces grew bigger.

Chapter 24

Clever, clever Ferocity. She was making me look bad. Unfriendly. Jealous.

That way, if I said anything – if I *did* say she was pretending to be an orphan – Lily and Kika would NOT believe me.

All that lunchtime Ferocity kept making a big show of trying to be my friend. But she was *not my* friend. I knew she wasn't.

Then the screecher rang for the end of lunchplay. And I trudged inside. Dreading the afternoon, dreading what Ferocity might have planned.

But that afternoon Mr Prankett walked into class and put a big bucket on his desk. "Emerald Class," he said, "this afternoon, we shall be visiting the Haggspit Museum of Witchhistory. And first — nametags."

We always wear nametags on outings. But not ones like these.

Because Mr Prankett tapped the bucket, and nametags flew out, then landed on the tables, in front of every witchkid in class. Each one with a name, a room number and a picture on it.

I looked at my nametag…

FLORENCE SKRITCHETT
ROOM THIRTY-SIX

…it said. And the picture was of an ancient manuscript.

I knew straight away what it was. The original manuscript of *Magical Myths of the Witchenlands*. The very first copy.

Lily had an engraving of the Battle of Bulging Bay. Kika had a giant's ping-pong ball. And Ferocity had a stuffed furzelgrunt.

"Find your match," said Mr Prankett, "and you find your partner for the afternoon." So we all started waving our nametags, looking around for our match.

"Snap," said a voice behind me.

I turned. Mervikk was grinning at me. Waving his nametag in my face.

Good. I was safe from Ferocity … for now.

✦

Haggspit Museum of Witchhistory is a huge old building – all big pillars and stone gargoyles, with stone steps up to the entrance. Steps so wide, so high, it's a real stretch for witchkid legs.

Inside, it has 347 rooms – including Room Thirty-Six.

"Find your room on here," said Mr Prankett, standing by the big museum map in the lobby. "Spend half an hour in your room, studying the object pictured on your nametag. Make some notes. Do some drawings. Anything you like."

Mamie's hand shot up. "Mr Prankett," she said, gasping. "Witchchildren let loose in a museum? No grown-ups with them? That breaks ALL the rules."

"Mamie," said Mr Prankett. "Would you like to see the Kronebay Tapestry?"

Because Mamie's picture was of a tapestry – seventy-nine panels, all showing a big battle at

Kronebay, sewn by witches a thousand years ago.

"Yes," said Mamie. Who is VERY keen on embroidery.

"And do you think you and Harikkon can find your way to the right room?"

"Of course," she said – looking a bit peeved at even being asked.

"Then you have thirty minutes, Mamie," Mr Prankett said.

Mervikk's hand shot up. "But Mr Prankett," he said. "I don't have a watch – not since I accidentally dropped it, then jumped on it. And Flo's not wearing one either. So how will we know when the thirty minutes are up?"

"Oh, you'll know, Mervikk," said Mr Prankett, smiling. "You'll know."

★

Room Thirty-Six was very dark. Just one light, glowing softly, above a big glass case in the middle of the room.

And inside the glass case – an ancient manuscript. Huge and old and tatty. Written out by hand in Ancient Witchspeak over five hundred years ago.

It had a label underneath it…

Witchmyth

Original manuscript of the book we now know as *Magical Myths of the Witchenlands.*

The manuscript was written in Ancient Witchspeak, the language first spoken in the Witchenlands around fifteen centuries ago.

Ancient Witchspeak continued to be spoken for ten centuries. But it was gradually replaced by the language we know as modern Witchen.

✦

This manuscript was translated by witchscholars over one hundred years ago.

The translation may not be entirely accurate, as the manuscript is in poor condition, and some parts are difficult to read.

The manuscript is written on paper made from trees in the Enchanted Glades, so is kept in a toughened glass case, under lock and key.

✦

The manuscript is very fragile, so please refrain from taking pictures.

Me and Mervikk stared down at the manuscript. It was huge, hundreds of pages long, with curled-up edges, and lots of spots of something all over the cover.

189

"Wow," said Mervikk in a hushed voice. "That is a BIG book. And mucky. And look. There's a blob of something – a great big blob. Covering up the end of that word there. That word in the title. The second word."

The Blob. The Blob Grandma talked about. I could hear Grandma's words in my head…

"…*those Shudders of Mummy's – they are not the only proof the myths are real. There is the Blob too. The Blob on the original manuscript…*"

I stared at it.

So – was *this* the Blob? It must be. But how could this Blob be proof of *anything*?

There was a button by the cage, with a label…

PRESS to see inside the manuscript

"I'm pressing it," said Mervikk, eyes gleaming. "It's on paper from the Enchanted Glades. It's an enchanted book. It might do something. Something might pop out."

Then his mouth turned down. "Although that case – it's very strong glass," he said gloomily. "So it's probably safe. Pity."

He sighed, and pressed the button. Inside the case, the pages slowly began to turn.

There was page after page of spidery writing. And paintings, astonishing paintings. A thrumbulger, rearing up. Dredgeboggles slithering through a swamp. The Oglestomp dribbling and – even crouched down – still tall as a giant gumboll tree.

And then – the Haggfiend.

Mervikk pressed pause.

She stared out at us.

Me and Mervikk stared back.

"She is NASTY," Mervikk said, with a happy shiver. Then he narrowed his eyes and looked thoughtful. "'Course – if she *was* real, if she came back…" he said, "she wouldn't go out and about looking for her little witchvictims like that. She'd go out in disguise."

Now Mervikk was thinking hard. "So – what sort of witch would she be, then?" he said. "One like Miss Boltsnip?"

Miss Boltsnip. Tall and terrifying, the worst supply witchteacher we ever had. Teeth sharp as daggers, which she gnashed all day long. And a serpent in her drawer, which she sent to twine itself round witchkids who annoyed her.

Then Mervikk's eyes narrowed more. He shook his head. "Nah," he said. "Not the Haggfiend – she's too sneaky to be a witch like Miss Boltsnip. She'd disguise herself as an ordinary witch, a lovely witch. One you'd never suspect. One doing good deeds, collecting for charity. A kind witchlady running a sweet shop. Even a witchkid."

Mervikk was starting to jiggle now. "That's it," he said, nodding. "The perfect disguise. She'd be a little witchgirl. Get herself into a school. Look around. Pick and choose her witchvictims."

I started making some notes about the manuscript. *Someone* had to do some work – and it didn't look like Mervikk was planning to.

Now Mervikk was moving on. "Although, if she came back she wouldn't be all that happy with that stinky old lair," he said thoughtfully. "Hundreds of years ago, maybe. That lair was probably luxury back then. But not now. A lair would be no good. She'd take one look at all the stuff we have, and she'd want it all. Skychatters, witchfixers, a nice house with running water. All sorts."

I couldn't stop gaping. How long was Mervikk going on?

Longer, it seemed.

He started jiggling more. "'Course, if she does come back, she'll be weak after all that sleeping. Need a bit of time to get her strength up, get her magic powers working properly," he said. "But when she does get strong, she won't just snatch a little Graciouswitch, I reckon. She'll snatch the palace, probably. She'll get a big army – all the horrible creatures in Witchworld. Maybe even nice ones too, but bewitched. Then she'll storm the palace. Take over as queen. After all – her mum and dad *were* royalty."

Now Mervikk's eyes gleamed. "Yes," he said. "Reckon she'll be FAR worse if she comes back. And grumpy. My dad is *always* grumpy when he wakes up – and that's after just one *night* of sleeping. Imagine how grumpy that Haggfiend'll be after hundreds of *years* of sleeping."

Then he had another thought. "And it's probably not that comfy, being disguised as a witch. That'd probably make her grumpy too. She'll probably have to change back into her own shape some of the time. And she's probably VERY smelly in her own shape. And—"

"Mervikk," I said. "Do some work. She is NOT coming back. First, she is not real. And second, even if she *was* real, she's in a cave, in an enchanted sleep. And no witch would ever move her."

"I would," said Mervikk. "*I'd* move her."

Then he pressed play again, and the page slowly turned. Another picture, this time the Haggfiend screaming in her lair. Screaming at a little witchgirl cowering in a corner.

Mervikk gulped. "Whoa," he said. "She is SCARY."

He took a step back. "Maybe I *wouldn't* move her," he said. "No. I wouldn't. I'd leave her be."

Then he pointed at her hair. "Look at that —" he said. "It's disgusting. All coiled and greasy, and it looks like it's writhing. And her arms. Long bony things. Imagine them reaching out to grab you. Imagine—"

But we didn't have to imagine. Because the eyes of the Haggfiend lit up. Glowed with flickering green flames. She started hissing. Then one bony arm started to push its way out of the picture.

And me and Mervikk jumped back as — snap! — the book shut tight.

We stood there, gasping. Then we both yelped. Our nametags had buzzed, and it tickled.

Thirty minutes was up.

Chapter 25

At the end of the day, Ferocity made her move. We were walking out through the school gates, Lily and Kika and Ferocity all chatting.

I felt edgy. Nervous. Because Ferocity kept looking at me, eyes glinting.

So I hung back. Tried to keep out of her way.

Ferocity did NOT let me.

She dropped back, and walked next to me. Then she opened her Haggspit Museum gift-shop bag and brought out a glass ornament. A tiny glass furzelgrunt.

"Flo," she said, eyes glinting. "Look what I bought

in the gift shop. Do you like it?"

I backed away…

But not fast enough.

Ferocity flung the furzelgrunt up in the air and let out a shriek – a loud shocked shriek – then threw herself to the ground.

Lily and Kika whipped round. Saw Ferocity falling. And saw the furzelgrunt spiralling up through the air, then down, smashing to pieces as it hit the ground.

Ferocity scrambled to her feet, eyes all big and shocked and wide. "Flo," she gasped. "Why did you do that? *Why?*"

Then she started making gulping noises, like she was trying to stop herself sobbing. "That was the first thing I've *ever* bought for myself," she gulped. "Orphans NEVER get to buy things."

I stood there, gaping. Gaping – and totally fed up. Because Lily and Kika were both glaring at me.

"It's not me," I said crossly. "She's doing it. Her. She's doing *everything.*"

Then I had an idea. I snatched Ferocity's bag off her. Opened it up. And there it was, tucked in the side pocket – the picture.

I got it out. "Look, LOOK!" I said, waving the picture in front of Lily and Kika. "She's LYING about being an orphan. This is her *family*. I know it is. Look how like her that witchboy is. He's her brother!"

I thought that would do it. That Ferocity would flounder, not know what to say, not know how to deny it...

I thought wrong.

Because Ferocity's mouth turned right down. Her lip trembled. Then, *actual* tears – two big fat ones – slowly dribbled down her cheeks.

"Give that *baaaack*!" she gulped, snatching the picture off me and holding it close.

"I dream about what my mum, my dad, might be like," she said – sniffing hard now. "I dream of having a little brother and a baby sister. And that witchboy – he *does* look like me. He looks VERY like me. That's why I took the picture."

Now she looked at Lily and Kika. Sniffed harder. Gulped harder, as *more* tears dribbled down her cheeks. "Maybe it was stupid of me," she gulped. "But I just couldn't help it. It was the first thing I did with my skychatter. I took a picture. Of that family. Strangers. Near Hurlstruk Happy Home. "

Then she turned. Stared straight at me with those big grey eyes. And now the tears were rolling – *streaming* – down her cheeks, and she began to sob.

"I was so happy being part of Clubbies. Having friends," she sobbed — right in my face. "And I've tried and *tried* to be your friend, Flo. But you just won't LET me!"

Then — off she ran, sobbing louder and louder.

✦

They fell for it. Lily and Kika both fell for it.

Lily gave me one ferocious glare, then went running after Ferocity.

As for Kika, she stood there, gasping. "Flo," she said, "what is WRONG with you?"

"Me?" I said. "There's nothing wrong with me. I keep telling you. It's all *her*!"

But Kika was shaking her head backwards and forwards. "Do NOT deny it, Flo," she said, jabbing a finger at me, and glaring. "All the evidence points to you having a very bad case of jealousy."

I glared back. "Evidence? What evidence? I am NOT jealous," I said. "Why would I be?"

Which was a mistake. Because now Kika started ticking the evidence off on her fingers. "One, she is a celebrity and you are an *ex*-celebrity," she said, frowning. "Two, she has lived on the streets and eaten raw gutter nibbets — which is more interesting than living in a cave-style self-build and eating a well-balanced diet. Three, she has a voice as good as yours — if not better, because there is an interesting tonal quality to her voice that I very much like."

Then Kika paused, wagged her finger. "Besides, Flo," she said, "there is all the pushing. There is evidence that pushing is your *modus operandi*."

I could *not* stop gaping at Kika. How much more rubbish was she going to talk? "My WHAT?" I said.

"Modus operandi," Kika said. "*All* criminals have a modus operandi, Flo — a way of doing their crimes. And pushing is your modus operandi. You pushed Ferocity in singing, and you pushed her just now."

Then Kika did MORE finger wagging. "Flo," she said, with a disappointed look on her face. "There are witchgirls I would *expect* to behave like this. But, Flo, you are not normally that sort of witchgirl. This is mean-spirited. Jealous. It really is *not* like you."

I spluttered. I felt my mouth drop open. I could hardly speak. How could Kika be such an idiot?

"It's not *like* me, because it's *not* me," I said.

But Kika was shaking her head, harder now. "Flo," she said. "It is not *fair* to try and blame Ferocity. A poor orphan — whose only crime is that she is trying to be your friend."

Enough. I did NOT want to hear any more. "This is like the possenfloff incident," I snapped. "Remember that?"

"Yes, I do," Kika said, eyes popping. "And this is NOT like the possenfloff incident."

"It *is*," I said. "And you had more sense when you were six – SIX! – than you have now."

Then I stomped off, alone.

✦

The possenfloff incident happened on a school trip to Haggspit City Farm.

Me and Kika were in a three with Mamie Swip. All sitting on hay bales, all about to pat a possenfloff – which, if you don't know, are related to windsniffers. Only much smaller, much fluffier and much MUCH cuter.

So we sat in a row. Kika, then me, then Mamie. Quivering with excitement as the keeper handed us each a small, stripy possenfloff.

Mine was curled up quietly, half asleep – little wisps of smoke coming out of its three tiny nostrils.

Kika's was snoring. Making three perfect smoke rings with each tiny snore.

But Mamie's wriggled and wriggled – then it jumped off her lap and ran.

Mamie turned. Glared at me and shrieked. "*You* did that, Flo!" she shrieked. "You POKED my possenfloff! You made it RUN AWAY!"

That was bad enough. But Kika sat there gasping. "Did you DO that, Flo?" she gasped. "That was *mean*!"

"But…" I said. "I didn't. I didn't do it."

"You FIBBER!" shrieked Mamie. "You *did*! I saw you do it!"

Then she made a grab for my possenfloff. "Give me YOUR possenfloff to pat!" she shrieked.

My possenfloff did NOT like being grabbed, so it started wriggling. And all the shrieking and grabbing woke Kika's possenfloff, which also started wriggling…

Then – both possenfloffs were gone. They jumped down, and ran away.

And Mamie and Kika sat there, shrieking at me. About how it was all my fault none of us had a possenfloff to pat.

Then Kika stuck her nose in the air, and tucked her arm through Mamie's. "I am NOT your friend any more," she said. "I am not being friends with a possenfloff poker!"

And they both marched off, and whispered all day about me being a possenfloff poker.

I went home so sad. Then I heard Dad knock on the front door and I ran to open it, mouth wobbling.

Dad scooped me up. "Why the sad face, Flo?" he said.

"Because," I said sniffing, "today was a very good day, and then it was a very bad day."

Dad sat me on his lap, and listened to my story. Then he looked thoughtful. "You know what, Flo?" he said. "Sometimes friends get it wrong. Make mistakes. We all do."

"But now Kika is not my friend. Not any more," I said miserably.

"If Kika is a true friend, she'll think about today," Dad said. "Think about you. What you're like. Realise she made a mistake. That you would NEVER be mean like that."

"But suppose she doesn't?" I said, curling up tighter.

"If she doesn't, Flo," Dad said, "then there are better friends out there for you than Kika."

"But I might not find them," I said.

Dad smiled. "Trust in yourself, Flo," he said. "Other witchchildren will always want to be your friend. You are true, and honest, and kind. And that is the right way to be."

Then he gave me a hug, and I felt much better.

And Dad was right. Kika *did* think about it. Because the next day she marched into school and straight up to Mamie Swip. Said I was not the sort of witchgirl who would poke a possenfloff, and Mamie was wrong to say I was, then try to steal my possenfloff. So me and Kika were friends again.

But that was back then…

And now, today, I wondered – would Kika do the same today?

Chapter 26

I walked home. Walked the whole way, feeling miserable. Usually, with problems, I'd talk to Lily or Kika, or both. But today, I couldn't. They *were* the problem. Them and Ferocity.

I let myself in through the back door, and got myself a shivershake. Then the front doorbell rang, so I ran to answer it. Maybe it was Kika realising her mistake. Or Lily, even.

It wasn't.

Not Lily, not Kika. But a grown-up witch on the doorstep. The neat, tidy witch with the big clumpy shoes – square, wide ones. Maybe she had big bunions on her toes, like Grandma has.

"I'm Malinka," the witch said, smiling a big stretchy smile. Then she paused. "And you…" she said. "You must be Flo. Florence Skritchett."

"I *am* Flo," I said – just as Grandma's voice boomed out across the hallway.

"Flo, I do NOT need a nanny! Send the witch away."

"I should warn you," I said, a bit nervously. "My grandma can be a bit … well – difficult. Stubborn. Grumpy."

Malinka smiled more. "Oh, I'm quite used to dealing with grumpy old witchladies," she said.

Just then, Mum came swooping out of her office and across the hallway to the front door. "Malinka, I am so happy you're here," Mum said. "Come and meet my mother."

Grandma was in her bedroom. Tucked in her shabby old armchair. She glared at Malinka, folded her arms, stuck her chin right out.

"Go away. Find some other witch to nanny," she snapped at Malinka. "One who actually needs nannying. Which I do NOT."

Mum sighed – and I gasped. "Grandma," I said. "Don't be rude."

But Malinka didn't seem to mind. She walked

over to Grandma, smiling calmly. "You have *no idea* what an honour this is for me," she said. "The chance to meet the great Dorabel Skritchett – ghoul slayer."

Grandma sat up a bit straighter.

"And I am *quite* sure you don't need a nanny," Malinka smiled. "But I imagine you could use a personal assistant – an important witchminister like yourself. I hear you are doing great things at Argument House."

Ten minutes later, off Grandma strutted. Ready to give Malinka a guided tour of the house and garden.

✦

My troll was behaving strangely when I went into my room. Padding around. All agitated. All bothered. Sniffing and growling and hissing. But I had no idea why.

Then his ears pricked up, his fur shot up on end – and he turned and ran. He ran straight up the wall and over the ceiling. Then he hung there, upside down, chattering his teeth furiously.

Now, outside my door, I could hear footsteps. And voices. Then the door opened – and there was Grandma. Behind her, Malinka.

"Malinka," said Grandma. "This is Flo's room."

That was when I heard hissing from above us. I looked up. My troll was hissing and hissing and hissing. Then he lifted one paw off the ceiling.

"No!" I said. "Troll! NO!"

I had a horrible feeling I knew what was about to happen…

I was right.

My troll sprayed. Green spray – stinky, smelly green spray. Green spray that shot all over my room, covering everything.

I clapped a hand over my mouth to stop myself choking.

I know about spraying from *Wild and Wonderful Witchglobe.* How trolls spray – often all over a witch's garden – telling other creatures to keep out, to keep away. That this is troll territory, not theirs.

Now my troll was baring his sharp little teeth, and bunching himself up on the ceiling. Then – growling and hissing – he hurled himself down on to the floor. And charged…

Straight at Malinka.

✦

A fluffy baby troll is not much of a threat to a fully grown witch. As he hurled himself at Malinka, she caught him.

"Oh dear," she said calmly, holding him in a good strong grip. "Someone is not very happy."

"Interesting," said Grandma. "Malinka, he thinks

you are an INTRUDER. He senses danger, a threat to his territory. He is guarding Flo, just as Otto did me."

I ran over. "Troll," I said. "Stop that. Stop that."

My troll looked at me. Looked at Malinka. Hissed.

"You really should learn some manners," she told him, then put him down on the floor.

I stood in front of him, my hand up like a stop signal. "No," I said. "No. You mustn't attack Malinka. She's not an intruder. She's living here, just for a while."

Then, from behind me, I heard footsteps, and Mum strode into the room. I turned.

"That troll," Mum shrieked, marching towards the window, "has to go. To GO! We canNOT have a creature living in this house who sprays our visitors! Who sprays our furnishings! It must go. Go NOW!"

She flung the window open. "Shoo," she said. "Shoo!"

My troll didn't budge.

"Very well," said Mum, and her fingers went flying, then she pointed her spellstick. "*Abrakkida Rune*," she said.

My troll lifted off the floor. He shot out through the window and landed in the garden.

He stood, glaring up at us, paws folded, as Mum

closed the window.

"Go, you silly creature," shrieked Mum, waving him away. "Go! We are setting you FREE!"

My troll did not want to be set free. He threw his head back, and he started to howl. To howl and to howl.

And – oh no… He set off the Howlings.

✦

Witches in Haggspit are fed up with the Howlings. Every so often one troll howls – and it sets off all the others. A chain of troll howls, spreading out across Haggspit.

Just like now.

Because now other trolls were howling back. Answering my troll, from all over Haggspit.

My troll looked astonished. Then he started howling again. Like he was talking to them, having a whole conversation. And, whatever he was talking about – it was deafening. Even blocking my ears, the Howlings got through.

"This is the last straw," Mum hissed, hands clapped over her ears. "The *neighbours*! What will the neighbours think? We canNOT have a troll here, in our garden, setting off the Howlings."

Now my troll was back again, leaping up on to the windowsill. Howling and hammering on the window. "He'll break it," Mum hissed. "Look! He'll break it."

She flung the window open again, and my troll stomped in. And – at last – the Howlings stopped.

Mum's mouth made a thin tight line. "I shall call in VapZappers," she said, getting out her skychatter.

I leapt over to her. Put my hand over her skychatter. "Mum, NO," I said. "Please. Not VapZappers. Not the Vermin and Pest Zappers."

I felt tears stinging my eyes. "It's my fault," I said. "I took him in. Please give me a chance to tame him. Please. Just a bit longer."

Mum wavered. I looked up at her. "I can do it, Mum," I said. "I know I can. And until I do, I'll keep him in my bedroom. Just in here."

Mum stared down at me. Thought. Then her mouth went into a thin tight line. "Flo, you have until I return to tame it," she said. "But no longer."

Then she turned to Malinka. "And, Malinka," she said, "if it sprays again, you have my permission to call VapZappers at once."

The grown-ups left and I crouched down in front of my troll. "I got you a present," I said to him, holding out a Haggspit Museum gift-shop bag.

My troll ripped the bag open and took out the present.

A book. *Groundgrabbers and Wallwalkers*. A lift-the-flap book. Full of all the magic machines witches use for building.

My troll stared. Then hurled the book across the room. So I sighed, and fetched him a shivershake.

He snatched the shivershake off me. But this time, he stuck the straw in the carton. Slurped it all down. Then he picked up Astribel's potty, marched off into a cupboard – and used it.

It was a start… But not much of one.

✦

Next morning – Thursday – Mum's bedroom door was open and I could hear her rushing around, talking to herself. So I went in.

Mum had outfits everywhere. Robes all over her bed, and the floor. She was staring, frowning. Scooping robes up, squashing them into a big heavy case. Pulling them out again. Muttering. Panicking.

She looked up. Saw me. "Flo," she said, panicking more. "The skycab will be here any minute. Any minute! I shall *never* be ready!"

And five minutes later, there it was. A big swanky skystretcher – ten-seater at least – landing in the front garden. With a driver in a dark-green uniform…

Wherever Mum was going, she was going in style.

The driver hopped out of the skycab and saluted, as soon as Mum opened the front door. Mum turned to me, eyes glittering and excited. "Darling," she said, giving me a big hug. "Work hard. Be good. I will be gone at least a week, maybe longer."

"Can I call you?" I said.

"Not for the moment," said Mum.

"Well – where are you going?" I said.

"Darling, I can tell you *no more*," said Mum mysteriously. "All will become clear, and SOON."

Then she left.

Chapter 27

Kika was already at the skybus stop that Friday. "One last chance, Flo," she said, straight away. "That's what me and Lily are giving you — but *only* because Ferocity asked us to."

She frowned. "So take this last chance, and use it wisely, Flo," she said. "Because on Saturday we are doing a Camping Clubbies sleepover. And we will be cooking Camping Clubbie Chowder over a Camping Clubbie fire. Then reading Camping Clubbie Chillers by torchlight in the tent. And it will be *fun*, and you do NOT want to miss it."

So Lily and Kika had talked about me, discussed

me with Ferocity. And they had talked about Clubbies, planned the sleepover – all without me.

I wanted to say something to Kika. But I didn't know what. Whatever I said, she would NOT believe me.

And Lily was just as bad. She stomped up the skybus stairs, sat down next to me and glared. "Do *not* mess up today." That was all she said.

So I sat there, silent. Glaring out at the clouds passing the skybus window.

How had things changed so fast? Last Sunday, me, Lily, Kika – we were all starting Clubbies, all looking forward to the new term.

And now... Now everything was wrong. All because of Ferocity.

I felt upset, fed up. More than upset, more than fed up – I felt *cross*.

How – why? – had my friends been so quick to believe Ferocity over me?

She was sneaky, a good liar and a VERY good actress. But even so, Lily and Kika – they should NOT have been so quick to believe her. They *knew* me. Knew I didn't lie. Knew I wasn't mean.

At least – I *thought* they did.

Then we got to school, and Ferocity came running over. "Flo," she said, grabbing hold of my arm. "Let's start again. Pretend none of this ever happened."

But I could see her eyes glinting. And I knew. She had more sneaky, scheming plans in store.

Well – I had a plan of my own.

I was going to put a stop to all this. DO something about it. And at lunchplay, I did.

As soon as the screecher went, I spoke. "Lily, Kika, I want to talk to Ferocity alone," I said. "We have things we need to talk about. Things I need to talk about."

Which was true.

Ferocity looked startled, but Lily and Kika both began to nod. And I knew why. They thought I was going to say sorry to Ferocity…

Which I was *not*. Oh no. That was NOT what I was going to say. Not at all.

So I marched Ferocity off down the playground, heading for the Hut.

★

The Hut is a small summerhouse with an arched opening at the front, and bench seats inside. It's at the far end of our playground, beyond the gripball pitches. A space for witchkids to sit. Somewhere to get away from all the hustle and bustle. To have a bit of quiet time.

And today the Hut was empty.

Good. This conversation was between me and Ferocity.

Ferocity followed me inside and sat down. She started swinging her legs. "Begin," she said, raising one eyebrow – an amused sort of smile curling up her mouth. "Say what you have to say. I am ALL EARS."

"Quiet," I snapped. "There's been enough talking from you. Now it's my turn."

I stood there, feeling cross. *Really* cross. Seeing her sitting there, swinging her legs – looking as if she found the whole thing funny.

It was NOT funny. "You," I said, "are sneaky. Very sneaky. And brilliant at lying. But sneaky is not something I'm good at. And nor is lying. So I've decided – what I *can* do is this. Tell you EXACTLY what I think."

I started listing things on my fingers. "You have *threatened* me – just because I am the only witchkid in class who is NOT fooled by you and your orphan story," I said. "You make out I'm jealous of you. You keep pretending I push you. You are ruining my friendship with Lily and Kika. And you have to STOP."

Then I glared at her. "So stop. Stop everything. Then we'll do what you said. Pretend all this never happened. Start again."

I glared more. "But before that," I said, "you have to tell me one thing. Why? *Why* are you pretending to be an orphan?"

Ferocity's eyebrows shot up. "Tell you why?" she said, looking astonished.

"Yes," I said. "You must have a reason – and I've tried and tried to think of one but I can't. Are your grown-ups horrible? Are they cruel? Is that it? Just tell me the truth."

"The *truth*?" Ferocity said, eyebrows shooting higher.

"Yes," I said. "You OWE me that. Tell me the truth – I won't tell. You can trust me. I'll keep it secret."

Ferocity's mouth dropped open. "*Trust* you?" she gasped. "A witchgirl? Keep a *secret*?"

"YES," I said, and I could feel my teeth beginning to grind. Because Ferocity repeating *everything* I said was getting on my nerves. A *lot*. "Trust me. I'll keep it secret."

Now Ferocity threw back her head and screeched. "Hah!" she screeched.

Then she started shaking her head from side to side. "There is not ONE witchgirl on the *whole* of the witchglobe who can keep a secret," she said, jabbing a finger at me. "Not in the Witchenlands, not in the Narrowlands, not anywhere. And that includes YOU. You might keep it secret, one day. Two days... Then it would be out. I know it would."

I gaped at her.

"Well, that's just stupid," I said. "There's *lots* of witchgirls who can keep a secret. You just don't know they're doing it. And I have NEVER told a secret. In my life."

"Liar!" hissed Ferocity.

I shook my head. "I'm *not* a liar. I never lie," I said. "I just can't. I have never EVER told a lie in my life."

✦

Now, I don't know what happened exactly, but me saying that – it was like something snapped in Ferocity's head. She started screeching at me.

"Ooh, aren't *you* Miss Perfect," she screeched. "Never EVER lie. Never EVER tell secrets. Never EVER done anything wrong. Never EVER made any stupid mistakes in your whole life! Never done anything you are *so ashamed of* you have to RUN AWAY!"

I gaped more. "So ... you ran away?" I said. "Why?"

Now Ferocity had started screeching, she couldn't seem to stop. "Not that it's ANY of your business but I did something so *horribly* wrong, I canNOT go home," she screeched. "I canNOT go back to Witchenfinn. My family are better off without me."

I felt something give a big lurch in my insides. Such a lurch I could hardly speak. "You think your family are better off WITHOUT you?" I said. "What could you *possibly* have done that makes you think that?"

Ferocity was glaring at me. "You *really* want to know? I'll tell you," she hissed. "I was supposed to be looking after my little brother. Except I was TOO BUSY. Too busy looking at cute clips of possenfloffs on my skychatter. Too busy to notice him – my own little brother – climb out of a window and up on to the roof of our house."

Ferocity's mouth started wobbling. "He fell," she said with a sob. And she wasn't acting now, I knew. She was telling the truth. For the first time EVER.

"He fell and he fell and he fell. I tried to stop him. Tried to save him. Tried to do araknawitchery. Tried to spin a web from my fingers, to spin strong thread all around him, to stop his fall. But I couldn't. Just couldn't. I wasn't fast enough. Wasn't good enough."

Ferocity had her head in her hands now. "And now," she said, "even now, after restoring potion – after lots of other potions – witchmedics still don't know if he'll ever walk again. Or speak. And it's all my fault."

She looked up at me. "So NOW do you see why I had to run away?" she said.

✦

Something was happening to me. I felt rage – fury – building up inside me. Up and up and up.

"No," I said. "No, no, NO. I *don't* see. I don't see why you had to run away. How can you *do* that to your family? Have you ANY idea how bad they'll be feeling? Not knowing where you are? What's happened to you?"

Ferocity flushed bright green. "I left a note. Saying sorry. Saying goodbye. Saying I knew they wouldn't want me as part of the family any more. Saying I'd look after myself from now on."

"A note?" I said. "A NOTE?" I was so furiously, so ragingly angry, I was surprised I didn't actually *explode*. I felt like I might.

Then I pulled a picture out of my robe pocket. The picture I carry with me everywhere. "See this. *This!*" I said. "This is my dad. My *missing* dad. And every single day, every single hour – every single MINUTE I think about him. Just like YOUR family will be thinking about *you*!"

I strode towards her. Grabbed her arm. Dragged

her off the seat. "You are an idiot!" I yelled at her. "You are the most stupid witchgirl on the whole witchglobe. But even though you're an idiot – you are *their* idiot. Your *family's* idiot. And your family will want you BACK."

Ferocity shook her head. Stuck her lip out. "They will NOT," she said. "Not after what I did. They *won't*."

"They *will*," I said. "They WILL. So go back. Go BACK!"

I felt rage like I had never felt before. Rage that made me want to yell and stamp and shriek my head off. Rage so strong I felt I could make doors rattle and windows shake. Rage that was about to boil over…

And get me in a whole lot of trouble.

Chapter 28

I tingled, I sizzled. I was so full of rage I could hardly breathe. And then – thick smoke started pouring out of my ears. More and more and more of it. Smoke that I could NOT stop.

And I knew – for the first time *ever* in my life, I had done fumawitchery.

Not Force 1 fumawitchery – tiny puffs of smoke, the kind grown-up witches, like Mum, do when their witchkids irritate them.

Not Force 2 or 3, or even Force 4 fumawitchery – those bigger bursts of smoke, the sudden ones that stream out then stop – the kind Hetty does when she's wailing at her nose in the mirror.

No. This was Force 7 fumawitchery. I was sure it was. My first fumawitchery – and I had gone *straight* to Force 7, the strongest fumawitchery of all.

On and on it went. Huge clouds of thick smoke, pouring out of my ears. Clouds of smoke heading straight for Ferocity, swirling round and around her. Worse, now I could hear buzzing. The buzzing of fumarons, attracted by the smoke. Buzzing that was louder and louder. So…

"Run!" I yelled. "RUN!"

Because the Hut has no door to close, just the wide open archway. The Hut was NOT a safe place to be. Not for Ferocity. Not with fumarons on the way.

Ferocity *did* run. She ran – surrounded by smoke – to the only place she could think of, the only place she knew she'd be safe. She hurtled out of the Hut, dodged round the side, and ran – just as the fumarons appeared in the sky.

A *huge* swarm of fumarons. Big and buzzing, antennae waggling, long sharp stingers bulging out of furry blue behinds. Fumarons – ready to attack. Ready to sting. Ready to take in big gulping breaths of the thick swirling smoke…

They didn't get the chance.

With three bounds, Ferocity leapt the fence into the school vegetable patch, hurled herself past the compost heap – and straight into the pond.

She landed in the water with a huge great splash. Then dived right under.

Just in time.

Ferocity was sent home in a skycab. Hauled out of the pond – covered in pondweed and muck – by witchteachers.

And this time she didn't have to act shocked. This time she really *was* shocked. By me, by the smoke, by the fumarons, by the soaking in the pond.

As for me, I was in trouble. BIG trouble.

I sat on my own, in a corner of Ms Riggle's office. Did work on my own. Had lunch on my own. Spent all day on my own.

Then – at last – the screecher went for the end of the day.

I walked out of school, down the steps, into the playground. All around me, I could hear witchkids giggling, witchkids whispering. Only one voice – Mervikk's – telling them all to shut up.

And there they were, Lily and Kika. Waiting by the gates.

"You are OUT of Clubbies," Lily said, glaring.

As for Kika, she just stood there, nose in the air. "I would rather prefer you NOT to take the same skybus as me and Lily," she said.

Then they both marched off.

*

Back home, Malinka was standing at the stove, sizzling something in a pan. Grandma was sitting at the kitchen table, stuffing bits of paper into a bright-purple folder with a big label on the front...

DOSSIER

"Tomorrow, Malinka," Grandma was saying, giving her Dossier a very proud pat, "tomorrow I shall strike once more. Catch that witch – that *scoundrel* – in one final crime! Because tomorrow Ariadne claims she is holding *Discussions*, Malinka. Discussions with witches from the Treaty Zones. Discussions on the outbreaks of fighting in Golmenn and Gelmenn."

Grandma gave a big sniff. "That witch will NOT be holding Discussions," she said. "She will be taking her grandchildren to the theatre. To an afternoon performance – a *matinee*, Malinka – of *Singalonga Spelltime*. I peeked in her handbag. Saw the tickets."

Grandma sat back, eyes gleaming. "But Edikk

will be there," she said. "Edikk will catch her! Snap her going in! And then my Dossier will be COMPLETE! Ready to present at Witchministers' Utterings!"

"Dorabel," said Malinka, "what a triumph that will be."

Then she turned. Looked at me, with that big stretchy smile. "Flo," she said. "How was your day?"

I tried to smile back – but I failed. I felt my mouth droop. "Not that good," I said. But I didn't say more. I didn't want to talk to Malinka about today. She was kind, she was nice – but she was still a stranger.

Then I heard the *putt putt putt* of a skyscooter, landing in the back garden.

Hetty.

Good. I'd talk to Hetty. Hetty knows all about falling out with friends. She might know what to do about a sneaky witchgirl. Give me some advice.

Then Hetty burst in through the back door. "News, Flo," she announced, grabbing me, and spinning me round. "I have News! This Saturday I am going away! On a witchdig! All weekend! Two days! Two nights! An actual witchdig! In Witchenwild!"

She clasped her hands together. "And Errken is going too! So there, on the witchdig – no signal,

no skychatters, no witchweb, nothing to distract!
— *that* is where Errken will realise that I am The
One!"

Then her skychatter beeped. "Gigi!" she said. "It's
Gigi! We're meeting on the corner. At Snak-Shak!
Outfits to plan! Strategies to plot!" Then Hetty
grabbed a brikkel from the basket on the kitchen
table, and stuffed it in her mouth.

"Back later!" she said, and she was gone again.

✱

I went to my room. My troll was sprawled in his
den, snoring and muttering.

I sat there, feeling worn out, exhausted. Something
about being so angry, so furious with rage — had left
me hardly able to move. Hardly able to think.

I had no idea what to do. About Ferocity, about
Lily, about Kika. About *anything*.

Then my troll woke — but the moment he saw
me, he hissed.

I felt even more miserable, even more alone. I
couldn't even make a troll my friend.

Time went so slowly that evening. Dragged on
and on and on. But at last, the suns started sinking
down in the sky, so I got ready for bed.

I went to close my curtains. Saw Malinka down
the garden, clomping through the gate from the

woods in her big heavy shoes. Back from a walk in the twilight.

Saw two faint flapping shadows above the trees. Shadows that looked like grizzelhumps. Flying over the woods.

Not just one – but two. I had no idea why grizzelhumps were here in Haggspit – were they lost, confused? – and I didn't much care.

I just crawled into bed and closed my eyes. Tried to shut everything out.

But that night, I had horrible *horrible* dreams.

Chapter 29

School on Friday was as bad as I thought it would be.

Lily, Kika – they wouldn't look at me, wouldn't talk to me. And Mr Prankett, with a grave, serious look on his face, made me and Mamie swap seats.

Then there was Ferocity. Still pale, still looking shocked. At first break, she followed me into the robe room. "Flo –" she said.

But I glared down at the sink. I could *not* look at her. "Do NOT say anything," I said. "Go away."

But Ferocity didn't go away. "I just wanted to—" she said.

"Go *away*," I said, and then I *did* look at her. I turned and I glared right in her face. "LEAVE ME ALONE," I said.

All morning I was miserable. All lunchtime too. I stood on my own in the playground. Witchkids still giggling, still whispering around me. And no Mervikk to talk to. Because Mervikk was ill, with a bad case of hurgles, off school until Monday.

I didn't think things could get worse – but they could.

Because that afternoon something happened. Something that changed everything.

✦

It was a treat, Mr Prankett said. We were having a treat for making it through the first week of term. A trip to the statue of the Haggfiend.

So we walked from school. Round Haggspit Harbour and up the winding streets to Haggspit Heights.

We walked up the stone steps – all three hundred and seventy-six of them. And there it was. Towering above us.

The huge stone statue of the Haggfiend.

Other witchkids – another school trip – were already up there. Lots of them, swarming around the statue. Groups of witchkids, posing in front of the huge stone hooves of the huge stone statue, taking pictures.

One witchgirl turned. She saw Ferocity, and gasped. She whispered something to her friends, three other witchgirls standing beside her. And – carried towards us by the wind – I could hear whispers. "The orphan… She's the orphan!"

Now all four of them were staring. Starting to walk towards Ferocity. And others too. Starting to crowd round Ferocity. Asking her questions, holding up their skychatters to get pictures with her.

And that was when it happened.

The feeling. The horrible feeling. A feeling I recognised.

A squirming, slithering feeling. A terrifying feeling. A feeling that started in my middle, and went creeping through every bit of me. Growing stronger and stronger. Worse and worse and worse.

Just like before…

When I Shuddered.

✦

No. I screwed my eyes tight shut. I squashed my hands round my head. I was *not* going to Shudder. I was NOT.

I wrenched my eyes away from the statue. I was going to *stop* those Shudders. Right now.

I filled my head with other thoughts. Thoughts about playing the firkelhorn. Magiography homework for Monday. My last holiday in Kronebay. Anything. ANYTHING to stop myself Shuddering.

But it was no use. I could *not* stop the Shudders.

Glimpses, scenes – through a swirling white fog. Things that flashed in front of my eyes, so fast.

Things flapping, things crashing, things falling.

Splashes of colour – bright blues and bright oranges. Sparks – small sizzling red sparks. And flames – flickering flames, all bright poison green.

I stood there, and I Shuddered. I Shuddered and Shuddered, as more glimpses, more scenes, flashed in front of my eyes.

A wide screaming mouth. Bony hands stretching out. And hooves, huge hooves. Huge stamping hooves.

And sounds, I could hear sounds. The sound of wings flapping. Cruel cackles of laughter. And shrieks, harsh shrieks. Shrieks of rage, of fury.

Then – screams. Screams that went right through me. Piercing screams... The screams of a witchgirl.

And that was when I screamed too. Really screamed.

As – *bam!* – I fell to the ground.

Part
Three

Chapter 30

I took Skybus 401 home on my own. Sat staring out of the window, thinking about my Shudders. Worrying.

What *were* they, those things I saw? Those glimpses, those scenes, through the swirling white fog? And the sounds, what were *they*? All those cackles, those shrieks, those screams?

And most of all – those hooves. Those huge stamping hooves. I kept coming back to those huge stamping hooves…

When the skybus landed, I waited. I wanted to talk to Kika. I saw how she looked at me after I

Shuddered. Knew she thought I was faking. Trying to take attention off Ferocity.

But I wasn't.

And I was scared.

Three skybuses landed, but no sign of Kika. And then, there she was – on the fourth. The doors swished open, and out she stepped.

I jumped up. "Kika," I said. "Those Shudders. I couldn't help it. They really REALLY happened."

Kika glared at me. I could see she was wondering what to do. Ignore me, walk straight on past. Or say something.

She decided.

She stood there, hands on her hips. "Right, Flo," she said, sounding all sarcastic. "So those Shudders – the Shudders that me and Lily have been trying to get you to do ALMOST EVERY DAY since the ghoul attack – they just happened then. Just as Ferocity was busy being a celebrity. A *celebrity*, Flo – which you were NOT being."

"*Yes*," I said.

But I could see Kika didn't believe me – and I didn't much blame her. Because Lily and Kika, wherever we go, they *do* keep trying to get me to Shudder, to tell them the future.

"Kika," I said. "I don't know why the Shudders happened then. And why not before. But they *did*. And Grandma says the Shudders are capricious. That they—"

But Kika wouldn't let me finish. "You know what I think, Flo?" she snapped. "I think that you did NOT Shudder – that you pretended to Shudder."

"I didn't," I said. "Kika, you *know* I don't lie."

"I know you *didn't* lie, Flo," Kika snapped, right in my face. "But I think you are now learning to lie. And pretending to Shudder is not a GOOD lie. Not a convincing lie. And that is because although you *are* lying – you are a beginner. And your lie is pathetic!"

She shook her head. Looked fed up. "You need help, Flo," she said. "All the things you've done – the jealousy, the attention seeking… You want my advice? Get your mum to book you an appointment at Upper Haggspit Medicentre."

Then she marched off up the road.

Back home, Grandma was hunched in front of her magic mirror – set to Roaming again, showing rows and rows of small pictures, constantly changing, of Haggspit.

I sat down. "Grandma," I said. "I got the Shudders today."

I thought Grandma would be interested – but she wasn't. Not really. "And what did you see, Flo?" she said, still staring into the magic mirror.

"I'm not sure," I said. "I squashed the Shudders down, hard as I could. I don't like Shuddering."

Grandma tutted. "The Shudders are *wasted* on you," she said. "*Such* a pity Hetty is not the Shudderer. She really would be FAR better."

Then Grandma sat forward. "There she is, Flo," she hissed, pointing. "There!" She waved her hands over the picture, and it grew, zoomed in. Until it filled the screen.

A skycab was landing. A skycab with four passengers. Three small witchchildren – and Ariadne Von Trinkpott.

"I knew it, Flo," said Grandma, eyes gleaming. "I knew it! There she goes. See! *See!* She is NOT in Discussions. She is taking her grandchildren to *Singalonga Spelltime!*"

Now Grandma rubbed her hands and gave a cackle. "But Edikk is in place," she said gleefully. "Edikk is skulking. Edikk is ready!"

"Grandma," I said, tugging her arm. "The Shudders, the things I saw … they scared me. There were flapping things. Crashing things. Falling things. And I heard noises – stamping noises, and horrible cackles. And a witchgirl screaming."

"Hm," said Grandma, tutting again. "Very little to go on. You really should try harder."

Then she leaned forward more. Ariadne Von Trinkpott and her three small companions were walking up the steps of a building. One with a big sign outside…

PROGNOSTIKON LANE THEATRE

"There's something else, Grandma," I said. "I saw huge stamping hooves."

"Hippaglomps, possibly – or unicorns, or gritterbacks. Any number of creatures," said Grandma, not sounding at all interested.

"It's just, those hooves," I said, "they seemed very … well – LARGE for a hippaglomp. And I wondered—"

But now Grandma sat bolt upright. Ariadne Von Trinkpott was walking in through the theatre doors, and – out of the shadows – a witchpap leapt. Snapped a picture, and was gone.

Grandma clapped her hands. "Well done, Edikk, well done!" she crowed. "Caught in the act! My

Dossier is now COMPLETE!"

Then she jumped up. "Malinka!" she called out. "Malinkaaaaa!"

And I heard the *clomp clomp clomp* of Malinka's shoes, then she appeared in the doorway.

Grandma beamed. "Malinka," she said. "It is done. I have a crook to unmask! A DOSSIER to deliver! Tomorrow, at Witchministers' Utterings! And you, Malinka, shall help me prepare. Prepare for tomorrow. Prepare for my great day!"

"Dorabel," Malinka said. "It will be my absolute pleasure." Then she smiled her big stretchy smile.

✦

I gave up on Grandma, and went to see Hetty.

"Inkompel, inkompel," she trilled. And, as I opened the door, she came leaping across the room.

"Tomorrow, Flo," she announced, "tomorrow is nearly here! Tomorrow, and my witchdig! With Errken!"

Then she swooped over to her wardrobe, flung it open and pulled out two robes. Held them up. "This, Flo? Or this?" she said. "Better to create an impression of great depth? Or great beauty?"

"Hetty," I said. "I need to talk to you."

Hetty waved her hand at her bed. "Sit, teeny, and speak. But be brief," she said. "Witchteen with

MUCH to do."

"I got the Shudders today," I said, sitting down on Hetty's bed. "At the Haggfiend statue. And I saw scary things. A screaming mouth, and bony hands. And I heard scary things. Cackles, evil cackles. And screams. Witchgirl screams."

Then I took a deep breath. "And, Hetty," I said, "one thing I saw – it was hooves. HUGE hooves. Stamping hooves. And I wondered if they might have been … well, *Haggfiend* hooves."

There.

I said it. I actually said it aloud.

Those hooves. Those huge stamping hooves – I said the thing that was worrying me.

I waited. What would Hetty say? What would she do? Would she gape? Cackle? Tell me I was an idiot?

No. She did none of those. Instead – she started wailing.

"You are SOOOO lucky!" she wailed. "Why isn't it me who Shudders? *Me!* Then *I* could see Haggfiend Horror. Me, not you!"

I gaped at her. Haggfiend Horror? What was Hetty talking about?

Hetty plonked herself down next to me, a jealous look all over her face. "I'd be *brilliant* at Shuddering," she said. "I'd see those myths clear as anything.

You know what myth I'd like to see most? The Oglestomp. Or dredgeboggles maybe."

Hetty looked at me wistfully. "You, Flo, you and Great-Grandma," she said, "you are SO lucky to have the Shudders."

Then she patted my hand. "It's a form of Confusions, Flo," she said, "seeing witchhistory and myths. But a good, harmless, *interesting* form of Confusions."

"Hetty," I said, "about the myths ... I, well, I just wondered –"

But Hetty wasn't listening. She was staring at her witchfixer. Then her face went pale green, and she started shrieking.

"I do NOT believe it!" Hetty shrieked, pointing. "Look. Look!"

So I looked.

Celebrity WitchWatch was on. The very first show of the series. The show where the cavemates meet for the first time. Where they go into the cave, one by one.

And a cavemate – cavemate number seven – was standing by the cave doors right now, waiting to go in.

A very glamorous witch. A witch waving and bobbing and smiling at the crowd gathered outside

242

to watch. A witch dressed in glittering green. Hair piled up on her head. A slash of dark-green lipstick, and a big confident smile stretched across her face…

Mum.

"Flo," said Hetty, grabbing me, sounding all panicky. "Flo."

Then her fingers went flying, she pointed her spellstick. "*Abrakkida Rune*," she said – and the volume turned right up.

The cave doors slid open and – to cheers from the crowd – Mum went inside. Not looking nervous, not one bit.

She swept down the staircase and swooped into the cave. Went straight up to a cavemate – a witchman in a very glittery outfit.

"You," Mum's voice boomed, as she pointed at him. "Lydon Skrimp. Tried to bribe the witchjudge in your divorce settlement. All hushed up, of course. But at *Hocus Pocus* we knew."

She turned. Looked at another cavemate. "As for you…" she said. "I forget your name – and the band – but you were the one with the looks but NO talent. Mimed your whole career."

Then she turned. Stared across the cave. "Ah-hah," she said, pointing. "Berken Groddswell. A little too fond of *shoplifting*, rumour has it."

I left Hetty with her head in her hands. Wailing once more.

"Tell me I'm dreaming, Flo," she wailed. "Please *please* tell me this is a nightmare and I will wake up. SOON."

Chapter 31

I went to my room, hoping my troll would be pleased to see me…

He wasn't.

As soon as I put my hand on the door, I heard him hissing. Then I heard the sound of scampering, scuttling feet.

I pushed the door open – and there he was, up on the ceiling. Crouched, and waiting. One leg lifted…

Ready to spray.

I shot inside the room and shut the door behind me. "Troll, *no*," I said. "It's me, Flo. Don't spray. *Don't* – or Malinka might call VapZappers."

Then I grabbed my dressing gown from the back of the door, and put it over my head. Just in case.

But my troll *didn't* spray. He stared down at me. Then put his paw back on the ceiling. Almost as if – now he'd seen it was me – he didn't *need* to spray. Knew I was no threat.

Good. That was a good sign. At least, I hoped it was.

And he'd been busy today, I could see. With a big box of my old toys I left out for him. Toys I thought a troll baby might like.

He'd been building with my bricks. He'd used my gel pens, done pages of scribbly drawings in my sketch pads – all drawings of trolls. He'd played my tambourine, my triangle and my maracas. He'd eaten all the snacks, and he'd used Astribel's potty.

Now he was scuttling across the ceiling, and down the wall.

So I crouched on the floor. Held out a hand. Maybe today was the day he'd come over, and say hello.

He didn't.

He sidled across the room towards his den. Then he leapt inside, and curled up in Astribel's cot. Started gnawing on one of my gripball shoes, staring out. Keeping a close eye on me – from a safe distance.

So I went and sat in *my* den.

Still worrying about my Shudders. Still trying to make sense of them. Work out what I saw. My Shudders ... did they see witchhistory *and* myths? Or only witchhistory?

Who was right? Hetty and Mum? Or Grandma? I just didn't know.

I switched on my witchfixer. There was something I wanted to do. Something I wanted to find out about...

The Blob.

The Blob on the manuscript in the Haggspit Museum. The Blob on that second word of the title. What was the word it was covering?

Mend ... that was all me and Mervikk could see of the word – the rest was hidden by the Blob.

So I called up the Ancient Witchspeak dictionary. Found twenty-three words that started with *Mend*.

Then I stared at two of the words on the screen...

Mendarikk: myth
Mendokkin: story

Mendarikk. That's what witchscholars decided the word was. *Mendarikk* – a myth.

But ... suppose the witchscholars were wrong?

Suppose the word underneath was really *Mendokkin*? *Mendokkin* – a story.

I looked on my bookshelf. At four books I have in the Story Series...

The Story of Hengitt the Hungry
The Story of Jeraboam Inkbold
The Story of Aragrit the Brave
The Story of Florazella the First

All four of them true-life stories... Stories about *real* witches...

So – suppose that ancient manuscript was NOT *Magical Myths*, but *Magical Stories*? True-life stories... Stories about *real* creatures...

No.

The Blob, the word being *Mendokkin*, that was just an idea. Not *proof* the myths were real. It wasn't.

But I thought more.

About the bones, the ones witchdiggers discovered. The ones that looked so SO like a thrumbulger...

And – out of nowhere – a thought popped into my head. A memory.

A memory of Grandma's doppel potion. The doppel potion she made when ghouls were around.

A memory of watching Grandma make it.

Watching her stand by her bubbling, steaming cauldron. Watching her drop one final ingredient – the hair from a doppel's head – into her potion.

A memory of how the potion *exploded*. How bubbles big as gripballs – black shiny bubbles – burst out of the cauldron. How they exploded all over the kitchen. Exploded like fireworks into big swirling shapes.

Shapes of dragons, and trolls, unicorns and griffins, serpents and windsniffers and gritterbacks. Hundreds of shapes…

All of them – every single one of those shapes – *real* creatures. REAL.

And one of those shapes – a thrumbulger.

No.

That was NOT proof. Not at all.

Those bones, Grandma's dopppel potion – they proved nothing. They were just more ideas. Not *proof* the thrumbulger was real. They weren't.

Yes, that's what I told myself. And that's what I hoped.

Because if the thrumbulger was real – then so were ALL the myths…

Including the Haggfiend.

So I sat there, worrying and worrying. Wishing and wishing I could talk to Dad, and then – the

Doubts crept in.

The Doubts are as bad as the Aches. Worse than the Aches. Because the Aches are like longing, but the Doubts are like fear. Like big terrifying thunderclouds swirling around in my head.

Doubts whether Grandma is right.

Doubts whether Dad will be back.

Doubts whether I will *ever* see Dad, ever EVER again.

No. NO. I was NOT going to think about the Doubts. I did NOT want the Doubts swirling around in my head. So I did what I always do when the Doubts swirl in.

I jumped up. Ran across the room, and pulled open my cupboard. Found my big black case, opened it up – and took out my firkelhorn.

My shiny silver firkelhorn.

Then I stood by the window, and I started to play.

I played one special tune. A tune me and Dad made up – one afternoon when rain was pouring down outside. Me playing the firkelhorn, him on the glinkle.

"This tune, Flo," Dad said, "it is yours and mine. Every time I play it, I will think of you."

So I played. I stood by the window and I played. I played and I played. I played until my fingers ached, until I ran out of puff.

Tonight I could NOT stop playing.

But the more I played, the sadder I felt. And the more the Doubts, like huge heavy thunderclouds, grew bigger and bigger and bigger.

Then, as I played, a small fluffy figure came creeping out of his den. Creeping across my bedroom floor. Creeping towards me.

And he sat. My troll sat. He sat at my feet, and stared up from the floor. Stared up at me as I played.

He sat, and he stared, and he listened.

Chapter 32

Next morning I got woken by noises. Scrabbling noises. The scrabbling noises of a small troll clambering up the side of my bed.

I opened my eyes, and there he was. Round and fluffy, and perched on the edge of my bed. He had a gift in one paw. A piece of dried-up old gum. He handed it to me, bright-blue eyes staring straight into mine.

"Thank you," I said, taking it. Although I had no idea where he found it — and I didn't much want to know.

Then he scuttled off to his den, and I heard

thuds and things moving, as if he was searching for something.

I opened my curtains. Outside, it was fine and sunny. Malinka was already out there. Heading down the garden, towards the gate into the woods, basket in her hand.

And here, in my room, my troll came scuttling back again. He handed me something – a book. The book I bought him in the Haggspit Museum.

Groundgrabbers and Wallwalkers.

So I propped myself up on my pillow, and my troll tucked himself into the crook of my arm. I opened the book. Then I showed him the first picture, and I started to read.

"This is a groundgrabber," I read. "It is an imm. An intelligent magic machine. Its big engine is full of dragon oil."

I stopped. Showed him the flap to lift, so he could see inside the engine.

My troll leaned forward. Lifted the flap. And gaped as the dragon oil bubbled and popped.

Then he crawked and he crawked, and he turned the page. Stared at the next picture. A big shiny wallwalker, crawling up a building. Eight long spindly arms stretched out.

"This is a wallwalker," I read. "It is a very nimble

253

imm. It can climb up the side of a building. It can paint and it can tile with its long thin arms."

My troll found the flap to lift. He looked inside. A little bubbling paint container.

My troll pointed. Stared. Jiggled. I thought he might burst with excitement. He could NOT stop crawking.

And that was when I decided. "Crawky," I said to him. "That's your name."

✶

Somehow – sitting there, stroking the soft fluffy fur of a crawking troll baby, looking out of my window, seeing bright daylight outside, and the trees in the woods shake gently in the breeze, I felt better. A lot less scared.

Whatever I saw with my Shudders – even if I *did* see the Haggfiend – there was NO proof she was real. None. Just ideas.

And even supposing she *was* real – which she probably WASN'T – and my Shudders *did* see future witchhistory… Even supposing that – there was NO proof she was back right now.

None.

My Shudders could be showing future witchhistory a long LONG way off. Something from years, decades, hundreds – maybe thousands –

of years ahead.

And maybe only a *possible* future.

Because the past is something that has *definitely* happened. But the future is something that could possibly happen.

Or maybe I Shuddered two ways. Saw future *and* past witchhistory. And those Shudders showed something from the past. Something long *long* gone.

Just then I heard feet hurrying across the corridor. My door burst open, and Hetty staggered in.

She had a big backpack on. Sensible shoes. Sensible robes. And specs slipping down her nose.

She gaped at me. At Crawky, propped up next to me. At the book. Then she got out her skychatter. "Gigi HAS to see this," she said, snapping a picture and sending it.

Then she plonked herself down on the bed. "This is it, Flo," she said, grabbing my hands, eyes shining. "This is IT! Next time you see me, I might have a boyfriend. *A boyfriend!* A boyfriend with DEPTH!"

Her skychatter rang. She looked. Gasped. "Flo, it's *him*!" she said. "It's HIM!"

She snatched it up. Answered it. "Errken, helloooo…"

And even though Errken was on the other end of a skychatter, Hetty was batting her eyelashes – up and down, up and down – under the specs.

"Yes, I DID read the article," she said. "Fascinating. Absolutely fascinating… Me neither – I never would have imagined there were so many ancient ogre axes in the mountains of Witchenwild… Yes, just leaving now… See you there."

Then she put her skychatter down and started shrieking. "He *called*! He CALLED!" she shrieked. "It is a sign, Flo. A SIGN!"

Then she gave me another hug – and was gone.

★

Me and Crawky went for a walk before breakfast. We walked down the garden, Crawky padding about – picking up things, sniffing them, putting them down again.

Then we went through the gate, into the woods.

Not many witches walk in this bit of the woods. I do though. I use the woods as a shortcut to Kika's. Because Kika's house backs on to the woods as well.

Kika never does the shortcut though. Not on her own. She says the woods are scary.

But they're not.

The woods are quiet, peaceful. They're called the Whispering Woods because that's what they do. They whisper. They're full of whispers. Full of tall trees with leaves that quiver and rustle, and sound like they're whispering secrets to each other…

They were whispering now.

And then – I smelt something. That strange smell. *Again*. Strong and spicy, but sickly and sweet.

Beside me, Crawky was hissing, growling, all his fur up on end. Then he crouched down. Started sniffling and snuffling along the ground, following some kind of trail.

He gave a yelp. Then leapt into some bushes and scrabbled his way through.

I ran after him. What made him yelp like that?

And there, in a small clearing, I saw it.

A windsniffer. A small windsniffer – standing totally still. Not moving. Just standing. Small piggy eyes staring straight ahead. Bristles all up on end.

I crouched down. Was it dead?

No. Things didn't die standing up.

Then – puff, puff, puff – tiny smoke rings came out of its nostrils.

But … *why* was it just standing there? Utterly motionless? What had happened to it?

Then I noticed something. Hoofprints. Right next to it. Deep hoofprints in the muddy ground.

Huge hoofprints…

I took a picture of them with my skychatter. And

a feeling crept up my spine. An uneasy feeling. A shiver.

The smell … the windsniffer … the hoofprints…

Now the words of "Haggfiend Horror" started echoing round and round in my head…

"*All creatures, all witches, rendered senseless by one look at her terrible face, by one smell of her terrible smell.*"

And suddenly, the woods felt all wrong. Not quiet. Not safe. Not at all.

So I turned. Starting walking. Walked faster, then faster still. Faster and faster up the path. Back towards the gate, Crawky following behind me.

I pushed the gate open, and I ran. Up the garden, and into the house.

✦

Back in my bedroom, I switched on my witchfixer. Those hoofprints…What *were* they?

I *had* to know.

The E list – that would tell me. The list of every known creature in Witchworld. And its current E status. Existing, Endangered or Extinct.

So I called the E list up on the screen. Uploaded the picture of the hoofprint from my skychatter.

Then I waited for the E list to match it.

Because the E list can match anything. A pawprint,

a clawprint, a pile of droppings, a poop pat…

Or a hoofprint.

The E list can say what it is. What kind of creature made it.

So what would this be? What creature made that kind of hoofprint? Whatever it was – the E list would tell me. And soon.

But the E list was taking a long time.

Long enough for Malinka to start clattering around in the kitchen. Long enough for cooking smells, breakfast smells, to come wafting along the corridor…

Much too long.

The E list must be struggling. Struggling to find a match for that hoofprint.

And it was. Because a message flashed up on the screen. A message from the E list…

NO MATCH FOUND

Just as Malinka called me into the kitchen for breakfast.

Chapter
33

Something thudded on to the doormat as I crossed the hallway. I ran to pick it up. The *Haggspit Herald*.

And there, on the front page – was a picture of Mum. Swooping down the *Celebrity WitchWatch* steps. With a headline...

LOCAL WITCH
STIRS UP A STORM ON
WITCHWATCH!

And underneath it said this...

Kristabel Skritchett, plain-speaking editor of *Hocus Pocus* and Haggspit resident, ruffled a few feathers when she entered the *Celebrity WitchWatch* cave. Last night ALL cavemates nominated her to be part of the first witchpublic vote-off.

Will Kristabel be the first to leave the *WitchWatch* cave – or will the witchpublic vote to keep her in? Full story, page 5.

I went into the kitchen and showed it to Grandma.

"See this, Malinka," Grandma said proudly, waving the *Haggspit Herald* in the air. "Skritchetts are once again headlines! And tomorrow – after Witchministers' Utterings, after I have unmasked that villain – it will be ME who is headlines. Headlines all over United Witchenlands. Quite possibly *witchglobal* headlines!"

"Dorabel," said Malinka, expertly flipping an omelette, "this is a day that will go down in witchhistory. A day that witches will NEVER forget."

"Indeed," Grandma said proudly. And her eyes gleamed. "Ariadne is due to speak at twelve," she said. "She is planning a big speech – about honesty and integrity among witchministers."

Grandma snorted. "Ariadne – honest. Pish! But

after that speech, *I* am tabled to speak. About ghouls. But I shall NOT speak about ghouls, Malinka. I shall present my Dossier. With every witchminister there to hear! That witch will have no chance to wriggle out of the charges!"

"Dorabel," said Malinka, bringing three plates of food to the kitchen table, big square shoes clomping loudly on the flagstone floor, "you will triumph."

"Malinka," said Grandma, sniffing suspiciously. "What is this?"

"Sweet and sour bikken balls," said Malinka. "Spicy tingels and pelloligan-egg omelette. A breakfast speciality of the Farflungs."

Grandma sniffed even more suspiciously. Then she took a mouthful. Chewed. Thought. "Malinka," she said graciously, tucking into her omelette. "You must give me the recipe. And this morning, you must help me get ready. You shall hear my speech, advise me on my outfit. There is much to do."

"Dorabel, I shall be honoured," Malinka said.

Then she turned to me. Stared at my untouched food. "Not hungry, Flo?" she said.

"Not really," I said, which was true. I wasn't hungry – not at all. I was worried. And I needed to talk to Grandma.

"Grandma," I said. "I found some hoofprints this

morning. Out in the woods. These."

Then I showed her the hoofprints on my skychatter. "And I checked, but they weren't on the E list," I said.

Grandma's eyebrows shot up. "Congratulations, Flo," she said. "You have found a new creature – a new species – in our woods. I shall alert the appropriate department."

She looked thoughtful. "In fact," she said, "I shall propose the government creates a further species status for the E list. *Entirely New* species."

Grandma nodded, pleased with her idea. "Yes. I shall propose creatures keep their Entirely New status for one whole year after their discovery. After which their status can become Existing."

Now, I know entirely new species are being discovered all the time in Witchworld. And that witchboffins reckon there are still thousands of species out there that witches don't yet know about.

But most of those entirely new species are small creatures. Bugs. Birds. Tiny reptiles. *Not* things with huge hooves.

"Grandma," I said. "That's not all. I saw something else in the woods. A windsniffer – not moving. Standing still, like it was frozen to the spot."

Grandma was nodding confidently. "That

windsniffer is suffering a SURFEIT," she said.

"A surfeit?" I said.

"A surfeit of grubbles," said Grandma. "That windsniffer has *over indulged* – as windsniffers do. A windsniffer is too foolish to know when it is full. As long as a windsniffer finds grubbles – it will eat them. Until it suffers a surfeit, and is too full to move."

Then she patted my hand. "Have no fear. The windsniffer will recover, Flo," she said. "Just as soon as the grubbles have worked their way through its system – and out of its rear end."

Was Grandma right? I wasn't sure. Because there was a look in that windsniffer's eyes that was … well – like *fear*.

Then Malinka pushed a big bowl towards me. "Try these, Flo," she said with that wide stretchy smile. "Wild glimberries. Picked fresh from the woods this morning."

But even though they smelt fresh, smelt lovely – I had no appetite. Just couldn't eat.

★

Back in my room, Crawky was sprawled in his den, snoring and muttering, paws clutching tightly on to his book.

I sat in my den. Stared at *Magical Myths*. At the

Haggfiend, screaming out of the cover. Tried to tell myself that Grandma was right. That those hoofprints were an entirely new species. That the windsniffer was suffering a surfeit.

Then I heard feet coming along the corridor. Clomping feet. Malinka.

She stuck her head round the door, and saw Crawky, sprawled asleep and snoring. "Safe for me to come in," she smiled. Then she walked into my room, and sat down beside me in my den.

"Flo," she said, "you seem unhappy. Worried."

"A bit," I said. "It's just … those hooves – I wish I knew what they were."

Malinka looked down. Saw the book in my hand. Saw the Haggfiend staring out of the cover with her huge stamping hooves.

Then she looked at me. "What does it say?" she said, pointing. "Right there on the cover?"

"*Magical Myths of the Witchenlands*," I said.

"*Magical Myths*," said Malinka, nodding. "*Myths*, Flo."

She stared round my den. At my pictures. At the picture of me and Dad in the story armchair.

"Is that your father?" she said, staring more.

I nodded.

"You look very like him," she said. "Same

265

eyes, same expression."

"That's what Grandma says," I said. "She says I'm a Valliant through and through."

Because Dad was a Valliant – Lyle Valliant. Until he married Mum, and changed his name.

"You must miss him very much," Malinka said.

"I do," I said. "Every day." And I felt my mouth turning down.

Just then Crawky started to stretch and yawn.

"My cue to go," said Malinka briskly, getting up. "So, what plans for today? Are you meeting your friends?"

I shook my head. "We sort of … fell out," I said. And I felt my mouth turn down more. I was just so sad. So worried. About everything.

"Poor Flo," said Malinka, walking to the door. "All alone."

In the doorway, she turned. "Flo," she said, "after your grandmother goes, we'll do something. Something fun. Just you and me."

"Thanks," I said. And I knew she was trying to cheer me up – so I tried to smile.

"I *promise* you," Malinka said. "I'll keep you busy. You won't have time to miss your friends."

Then she left and closed the door behind her.

Chapter 34

The next two hours dragged by. I sat in front of the witchscreen, and stared at Mum on *Celebrity WitchWatch*. Milking a two-headed grinthog to earn treats for the cave. Bossing a cavemate about in the kitchen. Yelling at the glittery witchman for stealing her lipstick.

But watching Mum made me miss her much more. Made me wish and wish and *wish* she was here. So I switched off the witchscreen, and went to my bedroom.

I tidied it. The whole thing.

Crawky would untidy it all, I knew he would,

soon as he was awake. But it was something to do. Something to try and stop myself thinking.

Thinking about the Shudders – the swirling fog, the flapping, the crashing, the cackles, the screams. And those hooves...

Thinking about the Haggfiend – *was* she real? Was she out there, somewhere in the woods, somewhere in Haggspit? I just didn't know.

I went to the kitchen, got myself a shivershake, then huddled down on the sitting-room sofa.

I stared at the magic mirror, still set to Roaming. Stared at the pictures.

At mermaids leaping in Haggspit Harbour. At fruit-picking imms working in the sloping skrumpel orchards. At goblins juggling, entertaining the crowds in South Siren Square...

And then – there they were. The Whispering Woods. One small picture Roaming through the woods, Roaming down a path I knew. The path to Kika's house. To Kika's garden.

And Kika was there. At the bottom of her garden, with her mum.

I jumped up and waved my hands at the picture. It zoomed in, and filled the screen.

Kika's mum was pointing her spellstick. And slowly, slowly, a shimmering magicreation was taking shape.

A cosy campsite.

A tent with big windows and, through the open tent flap, three soft sleeping bags lined up inside.

A cooking pot, hanging over a flickering fire. Blankets and cushions and little log seats scattered all around it.

Kika started beaming, and gave her mum a big hug. Then her mum left.

I sat there, more miserable than ever, and stared at Kika. She was wearing a new top – a Clubbie top. I heard them talking yesterday, planning to go to Genkel and Glimms. Planning to get matching tops.

Now Kika was pinning on her Clubbie badge. Then she looked up. She must have heard something.

She had.

Lily. She came walking down the garden. Wearing *her* Clubbie top, *her* Clubbie badge.

And I realised something. Both of them – they were looking very serious. Starting to talk. Shaking their heads. Looking cross.

I didn't think I *could* feel worse, but I did. Because I knew what they were talking about, what they were cross about...

Me.

Me – and all the things they thought I had done.

Then they both turned.

Now Ferocity was there. Walking down the garden, her Clubbie top in her hand. And Lily and Kika were walking towards her.

No.

I waved my hand at the magic mirror. Got rid of the picture. I did NOT want to see Camping Clubbies begin. See all the fun stuff they were doing.

Then I heard a voice behind me.

"Flo," it said. "My big moment is almost here! The most *important* day of my life! The day I reveal Ariadne Von Trinkpott for the villain she is!"

Grandma was ready. Standing in the doorway, eyes gleaming with excitement. She had her best velvet robes on. Her smartest pointy hat, a green feather tucked to one side. She looked pleased. Proud. Thrilled.

I felt a lurch in my insides. I ran over to her. I did NOT want Grandma to go. But how could I say that? Spoil her big moment? I couldn't. Just *couldn't*.

I knew how much this meant to Grandma. How important it was. And it was just a few hours. A few hours, that was all – and she'd be back.

"Good luck, Grandma," I said, giving her a hug. And then, I just couldn't help saying, "But please, *please*, come back soon." And I hugged her tighter.

Grandma hugged me back. Then she pushed me away. Stared at me. Peered through her specs. Frowned. "Flo. Something is wrong," she said. "I can feel you tremble. Sense your fear."

She peered closer. "Are you … *scared*?" she said. "Is there something you wish to tell me?"

"Yes… No… I don't know," I said.

Malinka came in, carrying a big bag. Grandma's bag, with the Dossier poking out. "Dorabel," she said. "Look at the time. You *must* go."

But Grandma stood there, staring at me. As if, suddenly, she was realising something. "Flo, you are truly worried," she said. "Truly *fearful*. I can see it."

"Grandma, it's OK," I said. "There *is* something I want to talk to you about. But it can wait until you get back."

And it could. Now was not the time to tell Grandma how scared I was. That the Haggfiend might be real, might be back. That I saw her with my Shudders.

Not just as Grandma's big moment was here.

But now Grandma was shaking her head. Looking cross – cross with herself. "Flo," she said. "I have been a foolish old witch. Selfish. Too busy with my own arrangements to notice you. You – with no mother here, no Henrietta. I have neglected you. Failed to pay you attention."

She patted me on the shoulder. "When I get back, we shall sit and talk," she said. "You shall tell me of your fears. And we shall bake together, a feast of iced kringels. You and me. Then we shall sit and eat them, cosy and warm in front of the fire."

✦

I watched Grandma and Malinka from the sitting room window. Both out in the back garden, Grandma clambering on to her broomstick, Malinka standing close by.

Then I saw them – grizzelhumps.

Grizzelhumps, in the woods, the Whispering Woods.

Not just one grizzelhump, but two, three, four, more… Grizzelhumps gathering. Gathering in the trees, in the woods – *our* woods.

Grizzelhumps…

I thought of *Magical Myths*, of "Haggfiend Horror" – of what it said…

"*For the Haggfiend gathered around her flying humped creatures. Mild of manner and simple of brain – and bewitched by one stare from the Haggfiend's eyes.*"

I felt chills creeping through me.

Grizzelhumps … flying humped creatures…

Why were grizzelhumps gathering? Why *now*? And why *here*? Why so close by?

I watched Malinka helping Grandma with her bag. Saw her urging Grandma to hurry.

And – out of nowhere – Mervikk's voice started echoing round in my head...

"... *she'd be in disguise ... some ordinary witch, a lovely witch. One you'd never suspect.*"

I thought of my walk in the woods this morning. Of that smell. The hoofprints. The windsniffer. And, once more, I could hear Mervikk's voice...

"*She'll have to change back into her own shape some of the time...*"

And I thought of Malinka. Malinka, at the kitchen table this morning, pushing the big bowl towards me. What she'd said...

"*Wild glimberries. Picked fresh from the woods this morning.*"

The woods – Malinka had been down in the woods. Earlier this morning.

Then I heard something. The sound of a door handle rattling on the other side of the house. My bedroom door handle. Rattling and rattling and rattling, as if something was trying desperately to get out.

Something did. I heard scampering paws. Paws

slipping and sliding and slithering on the wooden floor of the hallway. Paws heading towards the sitting room – fast.

And there he was. Crawky. Bursting into the sitting room. Growling and hissing, fur all on end. Leaping at the window. Scrabbling at the window. Scrabbling harder and harder and harder. Desperate to get out...

Then Grandma's broomstick started to take off. Started to slowly lurch up into the sky.

And Malinka turned. Looked back towards the house.

The look on her face – it made the hairs on the back of my neck all stand up on end. A look full of malice. A gloating *gloating* look.

She started to walk up the garden. Malinka, in her big clompy shoes...

Walking faster and faster. Up the garden. Up towards the back door. Up towards the house.

Towards me.

And that was when I realised.

It was *her*...

Malinka.

She was the Haggfiend.

Part
Four

Chapter 35

No. NO. Malinka … the Haggfiend.

Every bit of me started to quake. My legs, my arms, every bit of me quaked with panic. With terror. Sheer TERROR.

Because Mum, Hetty, Grandma – they were all gone.

And I was alone. Alone in the house with the Haggfiend.

I heard a creak. The creak of the back door opening. Then Malinka's voice calling out. "Flo," she called. "Flo. Where are you?"

Now footsteps, heavy footsteps, were clomping

across the kitchen. Clomp clomp clomp. Heading for the hallway…

Heading for me.

I ran. Fast as my quaking legs would let me. Out of the sitting room, and across the hallway. I grabbed Grandma's spare broomstick, propped up by the front door, then hurled the door open.

I *had* to get away. Get away from the house, get away from Malinka. NOW. I sprinted down the front steps, then clambered on to the broomstick. I clung on tight with my hands, and gave it a squeeze with both knees.

"Please, please, broomstick, take off," I begged it. "Please – before she finds me."

The broomstick wobbled, it wavered, it pointed itself upwards. And it almost took off … but not quite.

"I know I'm a learner," I begged it. "I know you get cross with me. I know sometimes you throw me off for bad flying. But today, now, please, *please* – HELP me."

But then – more footsteps, faster footsteps. The clomp of heavy shoes on the flagstone floor of the hallway. "Flo, Flo," Malinka was calling – much louder now – sounding puzzled. "Where are you? Are you outside?"

"Hurry, hurry," I begged, looking over my shoulder, and panicking. "She's almost at the front door. Almost outside. Almost here."

And at last – the broomstick took off. Left the ground, and wobbled upwards. One metre, two, three…

I clung on, terrified I might fall off. Terrified Malinka would come leaping out of the front door and grab me.

But slowly, slowly, the ground grew further away. The drop grew bigger. And we were off. Wobbling round the side of the house and into the back garden.

Then, from behind me, I heard a faint cry, a furious cry. Malinka. "Flo," she called. "What are you *doing*? Where are you *going*? Come BACK!"

No. I was NOT going back. *Never*. Not while Malinka was there.

I wobbled and swerved down the garden, then over the gate. I leaned to one side, and the broomstick turned. Pointed itself into the woods.

I swerved through the trees. Panicking.

Think, think! I told myself. Where to go? What to do?

But I had no idea. I was alone. So alone…

Too alone.

That was it – I was *too* alone. The woods were a *mistake*. The woods were the WRONG place to be. I needed to go where witches were. Not be here, on my own.

I leaned back, flew higher. Wobbled up through the trees. I had to get OUT of the woods. Go down the mountain, towards Haggspit Harbour. Go to places where witches were. Grown-up witches. Get help. Get witchwardens.

Witchwardens… Yes – the witchwarden station. That's where I'd go. Or maybe witchwardens would spot me first – a witchkid riding a broomstick. Maybe I'd hear sirens, loud sirens – and *soon*. Witchwardens on their way to arrest me.

Good. Let them arrest me. I *wanted* to be arrested.

They could lock me up. Sit me in a cell. Call Mum. Complain about her troublesome daughter. Riding a broomstick. Lying about the Haggfiend being here. Well – I didn't care. At least I'd be safe…

So I leaned back more, flew higher and higher.

I was almost level with the treetops now. Almost above the woods. Almost out of the trees. Wobbling and swerving far above the path I trod so often on the way to see Kika.

Kika…

No, no, NO.

There she was. Kika – far below me.

Kika *and* Lily. Two small figures walking through the woods. Walking up the path. Walking fast…

Walking towards *my* house.

But why? WHY? Why were they walking towards my house? What were they *doing*?

Every bit of me wanted to fly on. Fly up, fly away. Get out of the woods. But I couldn't. I *couldn't* just leave them. Not with Malinka around.

So I leaned, and I turned. Clung on to the broomstick and swerved, fast I could, straight back down.

I had to *stop* them. Warn them.

Down and down and down I flew. Back into the woods. Back towards the ground. Clinging on as the broomstick twisted and turned, and the ground came nearer and nearer.

Then – the broomstick crash-landed. Hit the ground with such force it hurled me off and into the bushes.

I staggered to my feet, reeling, dizzy. Ran out of the bushes. Ran on to the path. Ran towards Lily and Kika.

As soon as they saw me – they ran too. Ran

along the path, straight towards me. "Flo," Lily said, grabbing my hands. "Me and Kika, we were idiots. Wrong. And—"

"Lily, Kika," I gasped. "Run. *Run!* The Haggfiend. She's back! RUN!"

But it was too late…

Malinka was already here.

✦

She came stepping round the corner. Stepping down the path. Stepping towards us.

Malinka.

So calm, so capable, so cheerful. With her neat robes. Her neat hair. Her big stretchy smile. A smile stretched, right now, all across her face. Stretched from ear to ear.

A cruel smile. A gloating smile…

"Such an easy trail to follow," she smiled.

Then, from her robe pocket, she pulled out a wand. A wand that glowed a bright poison green. She pointed it straight at the sky, and words came hissing from her mouth. Ancient words.

"*Aborikkan Kidrioll, Okirria Haggunis!*" she hissed. And…

BOOM!

A thunderclap echoed round the woods. Then fog – choking white fog – swirled from the end of her wand. Smothered us, smothered her, smothered everything.

And, as the fog cleared – Malinka was gone.

In her place…

The Haggfiend.

Chapter 36

Nothing – no picture in *Magical Myths* – had prepared me for this.

The sight of the Haggfiend, towering, three times my height. So tall. So wild. So strong. With such a terrible *terrible* face.

I stood there, a voice in my head screaming, "Run, *run*, RUN!"

But I couldn't. The shock, the fear – they pinned me to the spot. Turned me to stone. I could NOT run. I couldn't even move.

And Lily, Kika – the same.

All of us. Helpless. Terrified. Staring at the

Haggfiend. Pacing around on her huge cloven hooves. Swishing her long spiked tail.

And the smell. That smell… Sweet and sickly, strong and spicy. So strong, so vile – it was almost choking me.

"I am *back*!" hissed the Haggfiend, her voice loud and harsh, proud and triumphant. "The powerful, the great, the MIGHTY Haggfiend! The finest sorceress that ever lived! One who commands the skies above. And the ground witches walk on!"

She stretched out one bony hand – long fingernails, sharp as daggers – pointed her wand up at the sky, then down at the ground.

And, swirling out of the skies, swirling down into the woods, the fog came. Choking white fog. Fog, swirling thicker and thicker. Fog, to keep witches indoors. Fog, to keep witches at bay…

The swirling white fog of my Shudders.

And now plants – stinking, oozing plants – slithered and twined their way out of the ground. They snaked all around us, they curled at our feet. Sharp thorns scratching at our trembling legs.

"Yes, the glorious Haggfiend is *back*!" the Haggfiend hissed. "Released by a swirling funnel of wind. A wind of vast power. A wind that swooped into my cave. Plucked me from my lair. And awoke me from my sleep. AT LAST!"

A windwhirl… It was a *windwhirl*.

No witch had released the Haggfiend – but a windwhirl.

The Haggfiend turned. Circled around us on stamping hooves. Stooped and sniffed with her huge hooked nose. Sniffing and sniffing at each one of us in turn. That face looming close – that terrible face…

A vicious face, cruel and evil. Cold hard eyes flickering with green flames. Hair writhing and wriggling with a life all its own. And a chin so big, so sharp, so pointed – it was a weapon in itself.

"Little witchgirls…" she hissed, "feast your eyes on the lair of the glorious Haggfiend!"

And – out of the fog – a shimmering magicreation began to appear.

A huge cave. Dark and sinister. Dripping and damp.

With spiders – big black spiders, bulging eyes shining – staring out from huge tangled webs. With serpents, tongues flicking, slithering and hissing across the cave floor. With bones of small creatures littering all the dark corners…

And a cauldron.

I stared. The cauldron – it was huge. Bigger than

the biggest cauldron I had EVER seen. Ancient and mottled. With a dark-green potion bubbling and steaming and brewing inside.

With a ladder, stretching from the floor to the cauldron's edge.

Thoughts – images – flashed through my head.

Thoughts of witchgirls – terrified witchgirls. Trapped and alone in the Haggfiend's lair. Climbing the ladder, quaking and quivering. Climbing to stir that bubbling green potion.

Shivers went through my whole body. Through my arms, my legs, all of me…

But *still* I could NOT move.

The Haggfiend dark mouth stretched out in a smile. She put her head on one side. "Little witchgirls," she hissed, "how do you like the look of my lair?"

She paced towards Kika. Stooped down. Squeezed her arm. "Healthy, well fed and *pampered*," she hissed. "Not a scraggy little witchgirl. Not one with diseases, and nits, and no flesh on her bones. Will you be a hard worker in the Haggfiend's lair?"

And I heard Kika whimper. A tiny whimper.

"As for you, little witchgirl," the Haggfiend hissed, in Lily's ear, "what skills can you offer the mighty Haggfiend? Will you feed my fine serpents?

Will you forage for maggots? Will you comb my long hair? Will you polish my hooves?"

Then she turned. Fury stretched across her cruel Haggfiend face.

"A *lair*," she hissed, "a LAIR is no good – not for the mighty Haggfiend. Not since I have seen how witches live *now*!"

She paced, she stomped, she swished her huge tail. "My mother was once QUEEN of the Haggs," she hissed. "My father was once KING of the Fiends. And I – the greatest of all the Haggs, of all the Fiends – I deserve far more than this *lair*! And I shall GET it!"

Mervikk – I remembered Mervikk. What he said...

"*She'll get a big army – all the horrible creatures in Witchworld ... she'll storm the palace.*"

Now the Haggfiend stooped down, leaned towards Lily, towards Kika. "Until that time," she hissed, mouth stretched out in a cruel curved smile, "you shall both have the honour of serving me in my lair."

"But make sure..." she hissed in Kika's ear, "NOT to *displease* me."

No. NO.

Not Lily, Kika. She could NOT take them to her

lair. And why them? Just them? Why not me?

Then the Haggfiend turned. Paced towards me. Stooped down, her huge hissing face close to mine. "Then there is *you*, Florence Skritchett," she hissed.

She stooped closer. "For you, Florence Skritchett, I have *other* plans," she hissed. "And now – I shall have my REVENGE!"

Chapter 37

I will never EVER forget how I felt. How shocked. How bewildered. How *terrified*.

Revenge? Why revenge? And why *me*?

"Hundreds of years I have slept," the Haggfiend hissed. "Hundreds of years of enchanted sleep. Tricked by a witchgirl – Kora Valliant!"

Kora Valliant.

Valliant… Dad's name.

The Haggfiend stamped closer. Nostrils flaring in her huge hooked nose. "Kora Valliant," she hissed, stooping down. "So disgustingly brave. So revoltingly good. She *tricked* me! Plunged me – *me*, the mighty Haggfiend – deep into enchanted sleep."

She crouched, huge haunches bristling, stared at me with those pitiless eyes. "I sniffed you out, Florence Skritchett," she hissed. "I would know the smell of a Valliant anywhere. That ancient witchgirl, Kora Valliant – she lives on through you. And I *will* have my revenge."

I shivered. Saw her dark-green mouth stretch out in a smile. A vicious smile. Cold and cruel, stretching right across her huge Haggfiend face.

"How well I planned," she hissed. "Your mother expected a QUEUE of witches for the great honour of serving Skritchetts. But there was only one."

She paused. "The other witches," she hissed – her smile small and sly, "I … *dealt* with them."

She leaned closer, eyes filled with hatred staring deep into mine. "I bided my time, Florence Skritchett. Weakened by years of enchanted sleep, I waited for my strength, for my full magic powers, to return," she hissed. "And then, at last, your mother – gone. Your sister – gone. And your grandmother – your strutting *ridiculous* grandmother – gone."

Now the Haggfiend bared rows of pointed yellow teeth. "So now," she hissed, "it is *time*. And I will have my revenge. REVENGE on the Valliants! You and I, we shall fly to the Kraggs of Kroke. To the highest of heights. And then – with one little push, I shall watch you fall. Down and down and down, into the Roaring Rapids below."

No. NO.

I could feel my fists clenching. A tiny clench. A tiny move. But a move all the same. My feet too. Every bit of me was beginning to move.

The Haggfiend's eyes gleamed. "So ... the fear that freezes, the fear that strikes on first sighting the Haggfiend, it dwindles," she smiled. "But too late for you, Florence Skritchett. Too LATE!"

She leapt up. Towered above me. "I shall *eliminate* you, Florence Skritchett," she said coldly, staring down. "Your sister too. And that will be an end of it. An END of the Valliants."

She started to cackle. Cackles of glee. Cackles of triumph. Harsh cackles, growing louder and louder.

Then she threw back her head, threw her arms in the air. "Creatures of the forest!" she screamed. "Come! Do my BIDDING!"

And – from deep in the trees, deep in the woods – a sound filled the air, cut through the fog. The sound of wings. Huge beating wings...

★

Out of the swirling fog, the grizzelhumps came. Huge humped creatures, orange wings beating.

Five, ten, fifteen … more. Swooping out of the woods, out of the trees. Swooping towards us.

One by one, they landed. And me, Lily, Kika – we cowered. Surrounded.

Now we could move. Now we could run. But it WAS too late.

The grizzlehumps towered above us, towered all around us. Giant birds, three times our size. With strong black feathers and huge orange wings. Long skinny necks and big bald heads stretching out towards us. Curved red beaks snapping open, then shut.

And those eyes. Those staring staring eyes, glinting and bewitched.

Bewitched by the dark enchantments of the Haggfiend.

"Trapped!" shrieked the Haggfiend, clapping her hands, cackling with glee. "Trapped! What now, Florence Skritchett? What NOW?"

Think, I told myself. Think, think. DO something. But what *could* I do? WHAT?

I'd had a plan with the ghouls. And Skritchetts to help – Mum, and Grandma, swooping in to save us. To save me, to save Hetty. But here … I had nothing. No Mum, no Grandma. No Skritchetts to save me.

And Hetty – she would be next. Next to be flown to the Kraggs of Kroke. Sent tumbling into the Roaring Rapids. Just like me.

I had *never* felt so alone. So small. So scared. So full of utter *utter* despair.

There was nothing I could do. NOTHING.

No plan. No Skritchetts. No one to help.

Just Lily and Kika, and me.

Me...

And my small stubby wand.

Chapter
38

My wand... Tucked inside my robe pocket.

Slowly, slowly, I uncurled my clenching fist. Slipped my hand inside my robe pocket. Felt the wand grow warm against my hand. Felt its warmth go right through me.

Almost as if ... as if – inside that pocket, the wand was trying to comfort me. Trying to tell me, "I am here. I can help. I helped with the ghouls. I can help you now." Then I heard something.

Howls.

Howls, muffled by the fog – but growing louder. Growing closer. Howls all around us, coming from every direction…

The howls of trolls. Urban trolls.

And then, the pounding of paws. Hundreds of paws, pounding from every corner of Haggspit.

Growing nearer and nearer…

And nearer.

"What is this noise?" the Haggfiend hissed. "These howls? This pounding? What is happening?"

Then – they appeared.

Trolls. Big trolls. Small trolls. Trolls with fur bristling. Trolls with teeth gnashing. An *army* of trolls. Swarming out of the fog. Swarming towards us from all over Haggspit. Howling and howling and howling.

And, right at the front, howling loudest of all – a small bristling ball of fur…

Crawky.

✦

Crawky leapt. He hurled himself straight at the Haggfiend. Then he sprayed. He sprayed and he sprayed and he sprayed – covering the Haggfiend in stinking green spray.

And all around us, trolls were doing the same. Hurling themselves at the grizzelhumps. Spraying and spraying and spraying. Attacking the grizzelhumps, as the grizzelhumps choked and flapped and panicked.

And the Haggfiend – she was staggering. Shrieking in fury, and covering her eyes. Struggling and struggling to shake Crawky off.

But Crawky would NOT be shaken off. Again and again, he sprayed.

NOW – *now*, as the Haggfiend struggled, as the grizzelhumps panicked – THIS was our chance. Our *only* chance.

So me, Lily, Kika, we ran.

Ran as fast as our shaking legs would let us. Ran back down the path, back towards Kika's house.

"Mum's not at home," gasped Kika. "No one's home. But we can hide. Lock all the doors."

"We'll call witchwardens," gasped Lily. "Get help. Get grown-ups. They'll save us."

So we ran. We ran and we ran. And as we ran, thoughts flashed through my head. Thoughts, one after another – faster and faster and faster.

Thoughts of Lily.

Lily teaching me how to dive like a mermaid. Lily shouting at Mamie for sniggering about forest pixies. Lily helping me pin up all my pictures of Dad.

Thoughts of Kika.

Kika giving me her shivershake when I dropped

mine in a puddle. Kika doing silly dancing to cheer me up when I had hurgles. Kika making me a special birthday box, all covered in sequins.

Thoughts of both of them.

Lily, Kika, both standing, both cheering, as I sang my first solo in the Haggspit Junior Choir. And today – Lily, Kika, both coming to see me today...

True friends, just as Dad said.

True friends who got it wrong. But true friends who were coming to see me, coming to put things right.

And *that* was why they were here. Here with me now. Running – so pale, so scared beside me. Running from the Haggfiend...

Because they were my true friends.

Yes, all those thoughts flashed through my head as we ran.

Then we skidded round one last corner and there, ahead of us, was Kika's gate. Kika's back garden. Kika's house.

"We can make it," Kika gasped, fumbling with the gate. "We'll lock everything. EVERYTHING. Then hide."

But already, from behind us, came the sound of huge beating wings. And the shrieks of the

Haggfiend, growing louder and louder.

She was on her way. Swooping through the trees on the back of a grizzelhump. Swooping down the path towards us.

Then, through the fog, came a shrieking voice. A voice full of malice, full of evil, full of hate.

"You shall NOT escape me, Florence Skritchett!" the voice shrieked. "Wherever you run – I shall FIND you!"

Then cackles rang out. Loud cackles, cruel cackles of laughter. Cackles of pleasure, cackles of glee.

"So run, little witchgirl," the Haggfiend shrieked, cackling once more. "Run, run – RUN!"

✦

And I *did* run.

But NOT through Kika's gate. Not after Lily, and Kika, pounding up the garden, towards Kika's house.

No.

Because I knew. A door, a lock – that would NEVER stop the Haggfiend.

And Lily, Kika … I had to get the Haggfiend away from them. Give them a chance to get help, to save themselves.

It was *me* she wanted revenge on. ME she would follow. Not them.

So…

"Come and get me, Haggfiend," I shouted. "If you CAN!"

Then I ran. *Away* from Lily and Kika.

I ran up the path. Up and up and up. Up towards the top of Moaning Mountain...

Up towards the huge stone statue of the Haggfiend.

Chapter 39

I ran. I ran and I ran, through the swirling fog, up the path, higher and higher.

Terror gave speed to my legs. Speed I never thought possible.

Because those Shudders, those glimpses, those scenes – I was beginning to understand what they might be.

And an idea, a plan, a TERRIFYING plan, was almost there. Almost within my reach.

So I ran, with Grandma's words echoing round and round in my head...

"*I do believe this is a one-witch wand... A wand that*

will work for one witch alone… In another witch's hands, this wand will backsurge…"

But behind me, the sound of beating wings was growing louder. Louder and louder. And a voice shrieked out.

"I am coming for you, Florence Skritchett," the voice shrieked. "I am ALMOST THERE!"

I turned – and I shivered.

At the sight of a grizzelhump, huge wings beating, bewitched eyes staring, was swooping closer and closer. And there, crouched between its feathered black humps, was the Haggfiend.

"You tried to escape me, Florence Skritchett," she shrieked. "But you *failed*! For I am here! I am HERE!"

Then the grizzelhump swooped towards me. The long bony arms of the Haggfiend reached down – and she grabbed me. Swung me through the air. Swung me up on to that huge humped back.

She threw back her head, and cackles rang out. Cackle after cackle of triumph, of pleasure.

"ONWARD!" she shrieked. "To the Kraggs!"

✦

That flight – that terrible *terrible* flight – it still haunts my dreams. Still wakes me at night, screaming with fear.

Me, clutched in the cold bony grip of the Haggfiend's hands. The grizzelhump wings beating and beating, as we flew through the trees, and out of the woods.

Then, looming ahead, there it was…

The huge stone statue – the magistatue – of the Haggfiend.

Nearer and nearer we flew. Higher and higher.

And I knew – *this* was what I saw in my Shudders. The crashing, the falling, it happened right here…

And it did.

That huge flying creature swerved. Swerved round the statue. Swerved to head north for the Kraggs.

But, as the grizzelhump swerved – the statue swivelled. Swivelled its huge stone head. Swivelled its huge stone body. Swivelled its long outstretched arm…

And the grizzelhump crashed straight into it.

✦

The force of that crash flung me away. Flung me in the air. Sent me hurtling up and up and up, then sideways, then down.

Down and down and down, until I landed…

On the long stone hand of the statue.

I clung on. Clung on tight as I could. Clung to its

outstretched stone finger. Wrapped myself around it, with one shaking arm. Tried not to look down. Tried not to get glimpses – through the swirling, choking fog – of the ground. Far *far* below.

Then I looked up. And there was the Haggfiend. Above me, wild-eyed and raging, crouched on the shoulder of that long – *long* – stone arm.

"I have CHANGED MY MIND, Florence Skritchett," she hissed, green flames flickering in furious eyes. "*This* shall be where your story ENDS!"

She came leaping towards me, sure-footed as the huge-hooved fiend she was.

I clung on, trembling, to that cold stone finger. Clung on as the Haggfiend came leaping. Brandishing her wand of bright poison green.

Now, NOW – *this* was the moment. And I had to take it.

I fumbled for my wand with one shaking hand. Pulled it from my pocket. Then pointed it, as it glowed in my hand. And the words came tumbling out.

"*Abrakkida Mutattikk, Bakkuliki Mutik, Diversikka! Optikka! Lune!*" I said, faster and faster. "*Ambik Non, Elsik Non, Revikkto Zin Rovvik, Ignittik! Bestolikka! Grune!*"

A shower of stardust burst out of my wand and swirled towards the leaping Haggfiend. And towards her wand.

She stopped. Shrieked.

"My wand! It burns me!" the Haggfiend shrieked. "It *burns* me!"

The wand fell from her hand. Fell from her long bony fingers. It fell and it fell and it fell. Then, far below us, with a spark and a sizzle – it was gone. Transformed…

And a buzzing red insect, long pincers flaming, flew off towards Haggspit.

The Haggfiend leapt, one last bounding leap. She crouched down in front of me. "What have you *done*, Florence Skritchett?" the Haggfiend hissed. "What have you done to MY WAND?"

She stared at me with flickering eyes. Eyes full of rage. Eyes full of fury. "No matter," she hissed, "for I shall use *yours*." And she snatched my wand … my short stubby wand.

"Hundreds of years I have slept," she hissed, nostrils flaring in her huge hooked nose. "Hundreds of years *wasted* – because of one Valliant. And now comes *another*. Another, who tries – ONCE MORE – to *defeat* me!"

She pointed my wand, bared sharp yellow teeth.

"Falling is too good for you, too easy," she hissed. "And so, Florence Skritchett, you shall SUFFER. Grow old – old as a witch of HUNDREDS OF YEARS. Grow withered, grow twisted, grow curled up and bent."

Her eyes flashed with fury, with flames of green fire. "And then, Florence Skritchett," she hissed, "you shall crumble to dust. You shall be *no more*. And revenge shall be MINE!"

She pointed to my wand. She screamed out the words of her ancient spell.

And a shower of stardust burst out my wand. Swirled through the air towards me – then turned and swirled back...

Swirled round and around the Haggfiend.

Chapter 40

She knew straight away. "This wand," she hissed, eyes flaming, "it does NOT do what I wish!"

She hurled the wand away, then clutched at her hair. Her writhing, wriggling hair. "My hair, my beautiful hair," she hissed. "What is happening to my HAIR? To me?"

She clutched at her face. "And my face, my skin – what is this feeling?" she hissed. "I am changing. *Changing!*"

And she was. Her hair slowly turning to grey, her skin beginning to sag, to furrow.

I clung on. Terrified of the rage on the

Haggfiend's face.

"My beauty – it fades. It fades!" the Haggfiend hissed. And now she was crawling towards me, her face ever more lined, more wrinkled, as she crawled. Palest green flames flickering in ageing eyes.

I tried not to look down, tried not to look at the ground so SO far away. But all around me, the fog was thinning, fading. Just as the powers – the dark enchantments – of the Haggfiend were fading.

Then she was here, crouching right over me. "You tricked me, Florence Skritchett!" she hissed. "Tricked me into using that wand. And you will be SORRY!"

She bared her sharp teeth, now rotting and black. "Whatever is happening to me, Florence Skritchett..." she hissed, "for you it is ALL OVER!"

Then she held out her withered Haggfiend arms. And she pushed.

✦

Now I knew. Those screams, the screams of my Shudders – they were mine.

I screamed and I screamed and I screamed.

I was falling, falling so fast. Tumbling down from

that huge HUGE height.

And now – from far below, came other witchgirl screams. Screams of Lily, screams of Kika. But still I plummeted downwards, faster and faster.

Nothing could stop me from falling. Falling and falling and falling.

NOTHING…

But something *did*.

Thread – strong and sticky. Thread that shot all around me. Caught me up. Wrapped me in a tight cocoon.

Then stopped my fall with one big jerk.

And there, far below me, was Ferocity. Pale, terrified – but spinning strong sticky thread. Spinning and spinning and spinning from her shaking fingers.

✦

I hung there, cocooned like a bug in a spider's web. Dangling from the outstretched arm of the huge stone statue.

I hung there. And watched.

Watched the Haggfiend fading. Growing hunched. Growing wizened. Growing shrivelled. Victim of the spell she had tried to do on me.

Watched her grow old as the oldest witch that ever lived, then older still. Until, at last – she crumbled to dust.

And I was safe. We were *all* safe. Me, Lily, Kika, Ferocity.

The Haggfiend was gone.

FOREVER.

Part
Five

Chapter 41

So that's it. The end of my very own Haggfiend Horror – but NOT the end of the headlines. No. The beginning of a whole lot *more*. Headlines like these…

FEARLESS FLO FACES NEW FOE!

FEARLESS FLO TRIUMPHS AGAIN!

Haggfiend Horror was the top story on *Haggnews*. Spycams up at the statue had filmed the whole thing. Filmed blurred shapes in the swirling fog.

The grizzelhump crashing, me, the Haggfiend...

They showed it all.

A witchhack from the *Haggspit Herald* wanted to interview me — but I said no. So she interviewed Lily and Kika instead. Which meant Lily and Kika were headlines too...

PLUCKY PALS IN HAGGFIEND ORDEAL TELL ALL!

Kika was thrilled. We sat in Lily's bedroom a week later, reading the article, looking at the picture of the two of them.

"Plucky Pals," Kika said. "Lils, we are Plucky Pals! Witchcelebs at last! And with a picture! A whole half-page picture!"

She gasped. "And who knows what this may lead to?" she said. "Maybe an important witchscreen director is looking at my picture right now. Pointing! Saying, that witchgirl — *she* must be my next star! Maybe stardom is about to BECKON! Maybe—"

"Kika, shush," said Lily. Then she clicked on her witchfixer. "I declare this Clubbie meeting OPEN!" she said.

Because me, Lily and Kika — we were friends again.

They worked it out in the end. Both of them, that Friday night. They thought about the Shudders, thought about me and what I was like. Thought hard. Then talked about it. Decided they got it wrong. That I would NOT pretend to Shudder. That I couldn't. Because the one thing I have never EVER done in the whole time we've been friends is lie.

"We should NOT have been fooled," said Lily. "We *know* you. Know what you're like. But we just sort of … forgot."

"We were hoodwinked," said Kika, who is learning a new word each day – *Ten top brain training tricks*, page 49 of the Book. "Totally hoodwinked. By a VERY good actress with an extremely sneaky modus operandi."

Lily just looked at me. Shook her head. "Flo, we were wrong. That's all there is to it. And we're sorry. VERY sorry."

As for Ferocity, Lily and Kika were planning to confront her when she came round for Camping Clubbies.

They didn't need to. Ferocity had done some thinking of her own. She had decided to tell them the truth.

Which she did.

She told them everything. About her, about me. Then she gave them her new Clubbie top, told them to give it to me, and left. She walked up the road to see me – to say sorry, say goodbye.

And she *did* see me…

Wobbling and swerving away on a broomstick.

She saw Malinka too. And heard the snarl she gave as I flew into the woods. She shadowed Malinka, followed her, then hid. And – just as we did – froze to the spot at her first sight of the Haggfiend. But when she recovered, she started filming. The grizzlehumps, the trolls, she filmed it all on her skychatter.

She sent it to the emergency services, told them where it was happening. But they spent so long arguing about whether the film was a hoax, they didn't get there in time.

And after Haggfiend Horror was over, Ferocity had her own headlines…

REUNITED! RUNAWAY BACK HOME
WITH FAMILY AT LAST!

I was right, of course. They were desperate to have her back. Not only that, but Ferocity got spotted by the Witchenfinn araknawitchery team. She's training now, with the Junior squad.

And her brother got better. Just one scar to show for his fall – a scar he's really really proud of, Ferocity says.

Because now Ferocity's stopped acting, I talk to her a lot. I'm even visiting her soon.

She's not Ferocity Hurlstruk, of course. Not any more. Her real name is Allegra Van Flint. But to me – she'll always be Ferocity.

Crawky was headlines too…

TINY TROLL A HERO,
SAYS GOVERNMENT

There was picture of him, with his paw in a sling. Because Crawky broke his paw, fighting the Haggfiend.

Witchmedics tried repairing potion, but what works on witches does NOT work on an urban troll. It turned Crawky purple, and made him HORRIBLY grumpy. So they made him a splint. Let his paw heal without any magic.

But because of what Crawky did – what *all* the urban trolls did – the government has made them a protected species. And witches have changed their minds about urban trolls. Now witches often tuck tasty bits of food and interesting rubbish into their wheelie bins, so trolls can have a really good scavenge.

And now that witches are much kinder to the trolls – now trolls don't have to scuttle and dodge, now they can pad along the street, chatting with other trolls – the Howlings seem to have calmed down.

Crawky's family are back too. They came padding up our garden – and Crawky hurled himself at them for a big reunion.

Mum's cleared out a shed for them to live in, and twice a week they come into the house, and have pomegranate bubble baths.

Not only that. Sometimes I go into Mum's snug and find her in there, with three troll babies on her lap, reading them bedtime stories.

Talking of Mum – yes, more headlines…

KRISTABEL SKRITCHETT CROWNED WITCHWATCH WINNER!

Mum was a triumph in *Celebrity Witch Watch*. The witchpublic loved her. Loved her straight talking, her taking no nonsense from any of the other cavemates. And the cavemates grew to love her too, in the end. Well, most of them.

The producers of *Celebrity WitchWatch* did tell Mum about me and the Haggfiend. They called her into the Confession Cave and showed her the footage from the skycams, and from Ferocity's skychatter.

Mum demanded to be let out. To leave the show. To go back home, and be with me. But the producers suggested I came to see her instead.

So I did.

Me and Mum had a private talk in the Confession Cave – no cameras allowed. Not one. Then I told her she had to stay in the show, and win it.

As for Grandma – she got her headlines too, just like she said she would…

DORABEL SKRITCHETT STUNS AT THE UTTERINGS!

I watched it all on catch-up. The huge room in Argument House. Witchministers lolling about on benches. Shouting, arguing, interrupting each other. Then – Ariadne Von Trinkpott. Standing up and making her speech. While Grandma sat there, arms folded, a big frown on her face as she listened.

Then it was Grandma's turn. She leapt to her feet, eyes popping, one finger pointing at Ariadne Von Trinkpott, and started bellowing.

"NEVER have I heard such twaddle," she bellowed. "Honesty, integrity – you, Ariadne, have NONE! And here – in my *Dossier* – I have all the proof that is needed!"

Argument House went wild. And Grandma was called the Hero of the Hour for uncovering such dastardly deeds.

But Grandma was not as proud of herself as she could have been – because of Haggfiend Horror. She came rushing home when she heard what happened, and sat me down.

"Flo," she said. "If I EVER get too busy to listen, too big for my boots again, you have my permission to *inform* me of the fact. You and your fears, you and your Shudders – I failed to listen to you. I failed to think. And I failed *you*."

As for the Shudders, I *still* don't know how Great-Grandma got them. Grandma says it's a long story – but I'm hoping one day she'll tell it.

✦

I was sitting in my room, thinking about the

Shudders, thinking about how I had to tell Dad about them. How they were *more* News.

Then I started thinking about how much other News I had. About my first fumawitchery. About Crawky. About my wand and the Haggfiend...

So much News. And Dad knew none of it.

And, as I sat there, the Aches started up, and the Doubts – both at once. AGAIN. And *that* was when Hetty burst in, eyes shining. Back from her witchdig in Witchenwild, right up by the Ice Volcano.

"Flo, I have *News*," she said, sprinting across the room. "Two bits of News."

Then, beaming, she gave me a big hug, and plonked herself down next to me in my den. "First news is this, Flo," she said. "I am going to Haggspit Museum of Witchhistory. With Errken. Who is not yet my boyfriend – because Errken is *cautious* and a two-day witchdig is not very long. But I think this may be a *date*, Flo. A DATE!"

Then she sat forward. Stared straight into my eyes. And her eyes started shining even more. "But, Flo," she said, "there is my *second* News. Much BIGGER, much BETTER News."

I gaped.

What kind of News could Hetty *possibly* think was bigger and better than going on a date with

Errken, than almost having a boyfriend?

Nothing could be bigger and better News for Hetty. NOTHING.

Unless … unless…

I looked at Hetty. At her eyes shining. And, deep inside me, something lurched. A tiny flicker of hope.

"We were staying in tents, Flo," Hetty said. "Tents right at the foot of the Ice Volcano. And there were caves there, full of snow trolls. And I heard them at night. Singing."

Singing. The thing snow trolls do best. You've probably heard it. Beautiful, beautiful singing. Unearthly, like something from another world.

"Flo," said Hetty, grabbing hold of my hands. "Flo – they were singing your tune. The tune you and Dad made up together."

I sat and stared at Hetty. She stared back, eyes shining and shining. "Someone taught them that tune, Flo," she said. "Someone…"

And still I sat. Still I stared. Because there was only *one* someone that could be.

Dad.

✶

So Grandma was right. Dad DID survive. The ghoul, the rocket, the Ice Volcano. He survived it all.

And Dad made headlines too…

IS THERE PROOF LYLE SKRITCHETT SURVIVED?

MYSTERY DEEPENS – WHERE *IS* LYLE SKRITCHETT?

I don't know where Dad is. I don't know why he's not back home – but I do know this.

Dad is out there. Somewhere out there. Somewhere in Witchworld. And I'm going to find him.

Yes.

One day I'll find him. One day I'll tell him all my News.

I *will*.

And I'm hoping that day will be SOON. *Very* soon...

What happens next?

Look out for

Witchwild